MURDER AT THE 10th HOLE

A ROSE BLAIR MURDER MYSTERY

JUDY KEIGHTLEY

Other Rose Blair Murder Mystery Novels

Murder at Bayfield Beach

Murder at the Croquet Club

Murder at Town Hall

Murder at the Marina

Murder at the Little Inn

Murder at the Retreat

Murder at Windmill Lake

Murder at Bayfield River

Murder at the Mine

Murder at the Winery

DEDICATION

This book is dedicated to all my friends who have supported me over the years with my writing. I thank you from the bottom of my heart.

PROLOGUE

Verdant grass glistened like a myriad of diamonds as the early morning dew caught the rays of the rising sun. At 5:00am in the morning, all was quiet. The car park was empty, the giant statue of a white squirrel seemingly standing guard over the entrance from highway 21 onto the golf course.

The manicured landscape of the lush greens stretched as far as the eye could see, the vista interrupted by small flags fluttering gently in the breeze marking out the locations of the 18 holes.

The normally welcoming, bustling patio of the White Squirrel looked almost ghostly at this unearthly hour with a thin white mist rising from the gravel that lined the walkways between the patio tables.

The clubhouse sat squarely to one side like a sentry on duty. Soon this too would be a hub of activity serving up delicious food to the hungry golfers and the passing summer tourists.

The earie silence was interrupted by the gentle purr of a car engine and a sleek, black Audi came into view travelling north along the deserted highway. It pulled off onto the shoulder some fifty metres before the golf course entrance and a tall lean, loose limbed man dressed in black swiftly exited the vehicle and hurriedly crossed the parking lot. Continuing between the new club house and the restaurant he stopped at the edge of the water feature, scanning the area beyond as if looking for something or someone.

From his pocket he drew out a small, collapsible telescope and using this he focused on the 10th hole. Jogging over to a clump of trees he once again drew out the telescope and, humming a little tune to himself, he turned and jogged back to where his car was parked.

Minutes later the Audi's engine roared to life and the car sped away back down the highway leaving the verdant green golf course to go back to sleep for another couple of hours before the crazy busy day of golfing began.

ONE

"OK, everyone, are you all ready for tee off?"

Tina McKenzie stood all five feet of her in the middle of a large group of women all dressed, and some over dressed, for a morning of golf. They were members of the White Squirrel's Women's league, and they met every Wednesday throughout the summer.

Amongst the crowd, Susan Parker, retired Chief Inspector Parker no less, and Rose Blair, both residents of the sleepy village of Bayfield, waited in anticipation of their tee time.

Rose was a reluctant golfer. She had been coerced into playing golf by her friend Susan who, having retired, not only from the police force, but from looking after her fiancé's egg farm, and her aged mother Olive, was like a prowling lion just waiting for some action.

Ironically, the thought of playing golf in her retirement had sparked a dormant interest, and Susan had taken on the challenge and thrown herself wholeheartedly into learning the game. Unfortunately, Rose had also been convinced by Susan that she should learn to play golf and now, after a month of practicing at the driving range, Rose had been talked into joining the Women's League and today would be her first full round of the season. Rose felt decidedly nervous.

Tina continued her spiel with a foghorn of a voice which was in striking contrast to her diminutive height.

"Remember to only tee off at your allotted time allowing for ten-minute intervals between each group of players. Also, don't forget to record your score on these cards." (Here she held up a small card and a pencil.)

"OK, we'll meet back here at the clubhouse at around one p.m. for lunch. Ladies, let's get started."

There was a gentle shuffling and sound of golf trolleys being dragged through the patio area and onto the pristine green turf. The White Squirrel Golf course was rapidly becoming one of the most sought-after golfing venues in the county. Formally known as The Bayview Golf Club it had changed hands in 2018, and now a beautiful and welcoming club house and meticulously groomed greens spread out before them.

A few of the women had opted for golf carts, but Rose and Susan had decided that the walk would do them good, something that Rose thought she might later regret.

There was a small commotion in the crowd as a young woman pushed her way through, calling out,

"Hey Susan, it's me, Mary."

Susan stopped in her tracks and squinted at the woman approaching. She was a gangly, sporting looking woman with long braided hair and a freckled face. She had an infectious laugh and as soon as she reached Susan, she wrapped her long arms around her in a bear like hug.

"It's been too long, what is it, maybe 20 years?"

Susan stood back and smiled as her recollection seeped in. She turned to Rose and said,

"Rose, meet Mary Malloy, my niece."

It was strange, Rose thought, as she had not realised that her friend Susan had any living relatives; she certainly had never mentioned her niece.

"Oh, it's lovely to meet you, Mary. Are you playing in this tournament?"

Mary laughed and said, "Oh no, I just like to come out with a friend and do a round of golf every now and then. I like to try out all the different golf courses in the area. Tomorrow, we're going to play the Seaforth golf course and on Friday I have a game booked at Woodland Links in Clinton. What about you two? It looks as if you're part of this group?"

Susan replied, "Oh, Rose and I have just joined the White Squirrel's Women's league, in fact, today is our first proper game of the season."

Rose pulled a face and Mary laughed.

"It's like that, is it? You know, my aunt Susan can be quite pushy if you let her."

Rose laughed and was about to reply when Tina called out their names for their tee off. Susan turned to Mary and said, "Let's meet up for a drink afterwards if you're still around. Shall we say at about 1:00pm?"

Mary looked at her watch and said that she probably would finish her game by then and would wait in the clubhouse for Susan and Rose.

She waved her hand and disappeared off through the crowds of women. Susan and Rose pushed their trolleys over to the first tee. They had been paired with another two women who introduced themselves as Helen and Lisa.

"Right, here we go, Rose come on, don't scowl, just enjoy the game."

TWO

Standing behind a small clump of trees about thirty yards from the tenth hole a man stood clutching a golf bag with a pair of binoculars hanging from his muscular frame. He was a lean man, over six feet tall and was wiry and athletic looking in an outdoorsy, rugged way. His skin was turned leathery, his hair was light brown laced with grey, and he had a very square jaw line. But it was his eyes that made him stand out. They were an arresting sage green speckled with yellow, like leopard's eyes, and just like the leopard, he too was ready to pounce upon his carefully stalked prey.

Picking up his binoculars, he homed in on a couple of golfers about to tee off at the tenth hole. They were two women, both in their early 40's, but it was the tall, lanky one with braided hair that he was focused on. He reached into his golf bag and extracted a rifle, a Tikka T3 plus Lite. Pulling the gun to his shoulder with practiced fluidity, the man steadied his aim and prepared to squeeze the trigger.

Just as the woman with the braided hair placed her tiny golf ball on to a yellow tee and stood up ready to swing her golf club, a sound like swishing-pop was heard and the woman dropped like a bag of potatoes to the ground. Just like that the life of Mary Malloy, niece of Susan Parker, was snuffed out, leaving her golfing partner, Jane, screaming out loud and searching frantically for some help.

The man with the rifle had already dismantled his rifle and was walking purposefully away from the clump of trees which had shielded his actions. By the time help came in the form of two other golfers, the shooter had already jumped into his car and was speeding away in the direction of Bayfield.

Rose and Susan were at the eighth hole when they heard the screaming. Up until then they had been having a good time and Rose had even begun to enjoy herself. At the onset of the screaming, they had stopped their game and were looking in the direction of the commotion. Rose said nervously,

"There was a noise that eerily sounded like a gun going off. Did you hear it, Susan?"

Susan, who like Rose, had heard what could have been the retort from a high velocity rifle, nodded,

"Yes, it sounded like a gun. Look," she pointed in the direction of the tenth hole where two men could be seen clustered around something indistinguishable on the ground.

"I reckon someone, or something has been targeted over there."

They could see one of the men speaking on his phone.

"Should we go over and offer our assistance?" Rose tentatively asked, but Susan shook her head.

"It looks as if everything's under control. No, let's continue with our game."

Lisa and Helen agreed, although Rose wasn't quite so sure. By the time they had reached the ninth hole, sirens could be heard getting louder and louder. Soon an ambulance appeared and made straight for the green followed by two O.P.P. cars. Rose, Susan, Helen and Lisa stopped what they were doing and watched as the paramedics bent over what was now clearly visible as a body and it was only as they lifted the person up onto the stretcher that Rose noticed the braids.

"Oh no, Susan, that's your niece Mary, isn't it?"

Susan shielded her eyes from the sun and peered at the body lying on the stretcher. The braids were not so noticeable now that she was strapped onto the gurney and being lifted into the ambulance.

"Are you sure, Rose? I can't even remember what Mary was wearing. I'm going to run over there and see if it's her."

Before Rose could say anything, Susan had set off at a singular pace and had covered the fifty or so yards from the ninth across to the tenth hole, in less than a minute. Rose smiled as she could see her determined friend arguing with the O.P.P. officer. She wondered what was being said. Susan ran up to the paramedic who was about to step into the ambulance and drive off. She shouted out to him to stop, and it was then that the O.P.P. officer stepped in.

"Excuse me, madam, what are you doing?"

"I think that's my niece you've just loaded into the ambulance."

The officer looked at Susan closely and then blew out a low whistle.

"Well, if it isn't DCI Parker. Hey, it's me, Sergeant Brown. Do you remember me?

Susan looked closely at the young officer and then a glimmer of recollection came. It was the mop of curly brown hair that had jolted her memory.

"Of course I remember you, although it has to have been a good four years. No matter, can you tell me what's happened here? I have a horrid feeling that my niece has been loaded into this ambulance."

Sergeant Brown looked serious, "Yes, well, ma'am, I shouldn't really say anything, but as it's you I will. A woman has been shot and is in critical condition. I'll ask her golf partner for her name, but right now the ambulance has to go."

With that the paramedic slammed his door shut and was racing off the green to Hwy. 21 with sirens blaring. Sergeant Brown turned to Jane who was being consoled by one of the golfers who had run to her rescue at the onset of her screaming. He said, "Miss, could you give us the name of your golfing partner, please."

Jane nodded and quietly said, "Mary Malloy".

Susan clapped her hand to her mouth. It felt unbelievable that barely one hour ago she'd been talking to her niece and now this monstrosity of a shooting had just taken place.

"Officer, you should mark where Mary was found and cordon off this area. In fact, you will probably have to close the golf course down for the day."

Sergeant Brown was taken aback by the authority DCI Parker displayed. She had been retired for some years now, yet she still sounded as if she was in command. Not being one to confront or ruffle feathers, the young Sergeant concurred to the retired DCI Parker. This had been a serious crime and as such would have to be reported to the Serious Crimes Unit in London and that meant DCI Whittaker, the slightly strange detective who had replaced DCI Hargreaves the previous year. He would have to be informed. Picking up his phone, he punched in the London HQ Serious Crimes number.

Rose, Susan, Helen, and Lisa sat underneath an umbrella on the patio of the White Squirrel. They were waiting to be interviewed by the police, but in the meantime, had ordered a round of drinks. Rose looked at the crowded area which now contained not only the Women's League ladies, but all the other golfers. The golf course was now empty of people, only the yellow police tape fluttered in the breeze at the tenth hole, disrupting the otherwise peaceful, pastoral scene.

They had been sitting there for over an hour before the sound of a motorbike drew their attention. Five minutes later a tall lanky man with red hair, holding a biker's helmet in one hand and sporting a leather jacket and biker boots, walked onto the patio. He looked very out of place, and for that matter, generally out of sorts.

THREE

DCI Jeff Whittaker's morning had started off alright until he had opened his kitchen cupboard only to realize that he had neither tea or coffee or, for that matter, any milk or bread. Jeff had not gone to the supermarket in weeks and now he was paying the price.

At least there were some frozen mice for Gengus, his pet Iguana. That would have really been a calamity if he had run out of supplies on that front. He could visit Tim Horton's for his own breakfast, but poor Gengus relied on him entirely for his.

Having received the phone call from despatch an hour ago he had jumped on his bike and driven straight over to The White Squirrel without stopping for his breakfast, hence his feeling out of sorts.

The crowd before him gathered on the attractive clubhouse patio, looked up expectantly waiting to hear what the DCI had to say. They were a mixed crowd, all women sporting golfing attire with various styles of baseball hats to provide shade from the already hot June sun.

"Good day, everyone. I'm DCI Whittaker and I'm from the Serious Crimes division in London. I have some bad news. The young woman who was shot at the tenth hole died a short time ago, and we are now treating this as a murder investigation. Sergeants Brown and Elliot will be taking your details and a short statement and then you are free to leave. As we will most likely be following up with some of you for additional information as our enquiries progress, please make sure you give my officers all your contact details."

Rose looked at Susan and could see that she was visibly upset. Squeezing her hand, she said quietly, "I'm so sorry."

Susan turned to Rose and said, "The awful thing about this, Rose, is that I never bothered to keep in touch with Mary even though she only lived down the road in Exeter. It's so ironic that I was genuinely pleased to see her again this morning and now I'll never be able to renew our relationship."

Rose nodded, what could she say to her friend, but she couldn't help wondering why she had been estranged from her niece?

"Had she always lived in Exeter?" Rose asked tentatively. As far as she knew Susan had grown up in Peterborough and she assumed that she was an only child. Susan had never spoken much about her family and Rose had never thought to ask.

Susan pulled out a tissue and blew her nose. Her eyes looked red and puffy, she was clearly upset, but she answered Rose quietly.

"Mary married a Mennonite fifteen years ago and was disinherited by her family. My brother was so shocked that his daughter had married Samual in secret that he refused to have anything to do with her or her new husband. Sadly, my brother died a few years ago and his wife, my sister-in-law remarried and moved to Toronto. My parents both passed away long before any of this happened and I lost all contact with Mary and her mother."

Rose asked, "Where did Mary live?"

"As far as I know after she married Samuel, she moved to his farm outside Listowel. I had heard some rumors about her leaving him but nothing concrete."

Did Mennonite women even play golf? Rose thought. Mary certainly did not look like a Mennonite although she did have her braided hair. "So, you don't know if she had any children?"

Susan frowned and then let out a deep sigh, "You know Rose, I know so little about my niece." Susan paused and then corrected herself, "She was almost twenty years my junior so by the time she was born I was away at Queens and then life got in the way. I do remember chatting to her at a family reunion way back when I was first married. She was always a rather peppy young thing. I do remember everyone being shocked when she became a Mennonite. Oh God, I was so looking forward to re acquainting myself with her again and now I never will."

They were interrupted by Sergeant Brown who plopped himself on the chair opposite Rose and Susan and opened his notebook saying.

"I have just a few questions to ask you both......."

FOUR

The black Audi sped along highway 21 passing through the hamlet of Saint Josephs and the Hessenland Inn on the left. Ten minutes later it slowed down as it approached Huron Estates Winery and the sign for Bayfield. The winery was relatively new, although it looked as if it had always been there nestled amongst the established vines.

The original owners, Renee and Allain, had moved to Bayfield from Orangeville and had built the barn-like structure housing the winery, over five years ago. They had planted over six thousand hybrid vines which were now thriving and producing tons of grapes.

Rose and Tom had bought into the winery two years ago after Tom had come into an unexpected windfall from an investment he had made in a silver mine in northern Ontario.

They had decided to put some of their money into Huron Estates Winery, and another chunk into buying a lovely home in Antigua. Consequently, they were now co-owners of the winery. But in a horrid twist of fate the previous year Allain had been murdered, leaving his widowed wife, Renee, to run the winery. Rose and Tom had stepped up and now all three of them ran the business together,

The Audi pulled up outside The Black Dog and the tall, suntanned man with the leathery skin stepped out and entered the pub. With a keen sense of purpose, he approached the bar and ordered a pint of beer and asked for a lunch menu. The bar man, young Andy, handed a menu over to the newcomer saying, "Just visiting Bayfield, are you?"

The lean man took a long gulp of his beer and said, "Yep, just passing through." He picked up the menu and glancing at it, pointed to the hamburger and fries saying, "I'll have that one." and, taking his beer in his hand, he ambled over to one of the tables against the wall and sat down.

A man of few words, Andy thought, but he had an interesting accent. He prided himself on having the ability to pick up where someone was from by their accent and this newcomer had intrigued him. As he put the hamburger and fries down in front of the newcomer, Andy casually said, "Will you need any ketchup or vinegar?" Leopard eyes looked up at Andy and spoke just two words, "Yes please." but that was enough for Andy to hear and nail the accent.

"You're from South Africa?" he said, barely concealing his triumph.

Leopard eyes said nothing and fastidiously ignored Andy until finally he left him to his food and ambled back behind the bar still wondering about the man's accent. He began second-guessing his original observation. Could he be Australian he thought, or possibly from Zimbabwe? He was about to go and have another attempt at conversation with the reticent man when leopard eyes abruptly got up leaving half of his lunch and drink on the table. He walked out of The Black Dog just as abruptly as he'd come in leaving a fifty-dollar bill on the table and a mystified Andy. Now he would never know for sure the nationality of this stranger.

FIVE

Rose pulled into the driveway of their lovely Bayfield Terrace home. They had built their house some eighteen years ago and planted lots of young trees to screen the property from their neighbours. As she stepped out of her battered Volvo the sweet smell of lilacs greeted her and despite a heavy heart her spirits were lifted by the sight of the four beautiful lilac trees all laden with fragrant blossom.

She opened the front door and was greeted by Ben, their very old and beloved black Labrador who hobbled to the front door with his tail wagging in greeting. Rose stroked his silky head, and Ben pushed his now grey muzzle into Rose's legs. The old dog was almost blind and now relied heavily on his acute sense of smell.

"Tom, it's me, where are you?" Rose walked through to their kitchen and opened the back door which led into the garden. Tom was hacking at the lower branches of the pear tree in a vain attempt at pruning the aging tree.

"Oh, there you are." Rose said, "Have you had lunch?"

Tom had become quite deaf, or sometimes, Rose thought, it was just a case of selective hearing. She stood there awhile longer watching her husband and thinking that he still looked pretty good for his age, and even though his hair was now completely grey he still had the ability to make her heart flutter when he looked at her in a certain way.

Tom stopped sawing the branch and turned, seeing Rose standing there.

"Oh hi, love, did you have a good game of golf?"

Rose shook her head and said, "I'm putting the kettle on for a pot of tea. Are you finished out here?"

Tom nodded and followed his wife into the kitchen, "You look tired love, everything alright?"

"No, it isn't." Rose fairly snapped. She had suddenly felt overwhelmed by the morning's events.

"What's wrong? Talk to me Rose." Toms face showed nothing but concern.

"Oh, Tom, Susan's niece Mary was shot at the tenth hole today. It was so horrid" she blurted out almost incomprehensively.

"Slow down, love and tell me again what happened."

Rose relayed to Tom the whole mornings sequence of events, missing nothing out. "So, you see, Tom, Susan hadn't seen her niece for almost twenty years and then she never got the chance to re acquaint herself."

"Did you say that she was a Mennonite?"

"Yes, although Susan seemed to think that she had left the order a few years ago, she was a bit vague. Honestly, I never even knew that Susan had any living relatives."

Tom was pensive, he finally said, "Why would anyone kill a woman so publicly?"

Rose had no reply, why indeed, she thought, as she poured the boiling water into the teapot. Why indeed.

SIX

Susan walked into her Harbour Court condo and was immediately greeted by her cat, Fluffy. Ian, her fiancé and the County pathologist, was at work and so the house seemed very quiet. She was about to make herself a cup of coffee when Susan looked out of her kitchen window and out of the corner of her eye, she noticed a piece of paper held in place by a rock on the little flagstone path that ran from the front of her house around to the side. She hadn't noticed it when she had pulled up outside her condo, but then she had been rather preoccupied with other things, particularly the murder of her niece Mary.

Susan opened the front door and walked over to the rock, lifted it up and grabbed the piece of paper that was under it.   Written in bold italic letters was **Book of Exodus 21 : 24.**

How strange, Susan thought as she examined both the paper and writing more closely. The words had been written on a torn piece of lined writing paper taken from the sort of exercise books that she had grown up with writing in at school. The words had been written with what looked like a black marker pen.

Susan walked back into her condo, closed the front door, and reached for her phone. She 'Googled' Book of Exodus, Chapter 21, Verse 24, and up popped the old commandment, an eye for an eye, a tooth for a tooth. What an earth does that mean, Susan thought as she grappled with the meaning and implication of the saying. Did this have anything to do with Mary's murder she wondered as she tapped in Rose's cell number and waited for her friend to pick up.

"Rose Blair speaking."

"Oh Rose, I've just had a very weird note left for me. Can I come over and show it to you?"

"Of course. I've just made a pot of tea, but I'll make you a coffee when you get here." Rose knew that Susan was not a tea drinker. She pulled out the container of scones she had baked the day before. They were not freshly baked, but they still tasted OK, judging by how many had already been consumed, Tom must have thought that they were alright. Rose loved to bake, particularly scones, but she really did not like eating them herself.

She grabbed three of them, cut them in half and smothered them with creamy butter which she had made the night before. Tom sauntered in and was about to take another one of the scones when Rose admonished him. "I've put these out for Susan, who's coming over. Can't you wait until then, Tom."

Tom eyed the scones greedily and then nodded his head. "They're my favorite love, lemon and cranberry."

Rose made a carafe of coffee and was just putting some cups, plates and serviettes on a tray, when Susan knocked on the door. Tom let her in and soon all three were gathered in the kitchen. Rose ushered them out of the crowded kitchen.

"Come on, let's go into the sunroom, shall we?"

Susan and Tom followed her into their cozy living room and into the sun lounge which was nestled at the back of the house overlooking the garden. Another month and then it would be too hot to sit in the sunroom, but right now, early June, it was absolutely just perfect.

"Come on, Susan, show us the strange note." Rose said while pouring out the coffee." Tom, do you want another cup of tea or some coffee now?"

Tom opted for coffee and then held out the plate of scones to Susan who took two. He then put a couple on a plate for himself and with a big sigh sat back onto his comfortable chair and devoured one of the scones in one whole bite.

Susan opened her shoulder purse and pulled out the mysterious note. "Here you are Rose". She handed the piece of paper over to her friend.

"**Book of Exodus 21 : 24**." she read out loud.

 Tom put his finger in the air and said, "I bet I know what that is, an eye for an eye, a tooth for a tooth. Am I right, Susan?

She smiled and nodded, "Well done, Tom. I had to Google it. But what does it mean? Do you think is anything to do with my niece's murder?"

All three of them were quiet while they thought about the implications of the note. Tom spoke first,

"This is all about retribution. Just who have you murdered Susan?" He said it with a twinkle in his eye, but Susan took what he said seriously.

"I haven't killed anyone, well at least not for years now."

Rose interrupted her, "But maybe it doesn't mean you personally, maybe when you were Chief Inspector? I don't know, it's all rather obtuse, isn't it?"

Just then the phone rang. It was Renee from Huron Estates winery. Tom answered. "Tom speaking."

"Tom, I have a doctor's appointment this afternoon. Is there any chance either you or Rose could man the tasting room. I know it's not your turn, but we could switch, and I could do your slot tomorrow if that works for you?"

Tom and Rose were scheduled to work 3 shifts a week at the winery. Between Renee, Rose and Tom, they somehow managed to staff the tasting room, although Susan sometimes helped out when they were busy.

Tom answered her straight away." Sure, I can do this afternoon's shift". Looking at his watch he realized that it was already almost two. The tasting room was open from two-thirty until six.

"Okay, see you later."

Rose looked at him and raised her eyebrows. "That's the fourth time she's rescheduled in the last couple of weeks."

There was no love lost between Rose and Renee. After Allain's death, Rose had become highly suspicious of Renee. Even though the killer had been caught and the case wrapped up, Rose still felt that Renee was not to be trusted.

"Oh well, it means I can play golf tomorrow with Doug, so that's OK."

Tom was so easy going and trusting, Rose thought. He had been totally taken in by Renee and believed Rose was just overreacting, but Rose had seen another far more sinister side of Renee after Allain was murdered. It was as if she really wanted him out of the way.

Susan looked over at Tom and Rose and smiled to herself. She knew exactly what Rose was thinking as she herself had also harbored suspicious thoughts about Renee. She loved to watch the dynamics between her friends whom she dearly loved. She had had an attraction for Tom whose easygoing nature had greatly appealed to her, but he was Rose's husband, and she would never cheat on her friend, besides, she was soon to be married to Ian, one of the mildest and gentlest of men she had ever known.

Rose turned to Susan and asked if she'd like some more coffee?

"So where were we before Renee interrupted us?"

"We were talking about that strange note that I found under a rock in front of my condo."

"Oh yes, you will have to contact DCI Whitaker I suppose, but it's very odd. Tom's right though, the quote I think is all about retribution. I reckon your niece's murder is in retaliation for the death of someone that you were responsible for, either directly or indirectly."

Susan nodded. "Yes, it is too much of a coincidence that the note should turn up just after my niece's death. There must be a connection, but quite where or what, is beyond me. I'll give DCI Whitaker a call."

SEVEN

Back in his small apartment in London, DCI Jeff Whitaker was sitting at his kitchen table with a plate of baked beans on toast in front of him. The kettle was boiling ready to make a pot of tea and Debussy's 'Moonlight Sonata' was playing gently in the background. Gengus, his beloved pet iguana, stood on the floor with his large head cocked to one side.

He was listening to the music and appeared absolutely raptured. Jeff looked down at his pet and smiled. Although most people would be horrified at having a pet iguana, Gengus had proved to be a great companion to Jeff. They both shared a love of classical music, and Jeff felt content with his status as a single person.

Jeff had been married to Ann, his ex-wife, and lived in Peterborough for five years until they separated and then divorced. Since moving to London after joining the Serious Crimes

Unit, he had learned that living on one's own was okay. That had been almost two years ago now and he had got to enjoy his own company and that of his pet Gengus.

"Are you ready for some lunch, mate?" Jeff said between mouthfuls of baked beans." I've got some lovely mice for you."

He had called in at the pet store on his way back from Bayfield and had picked up a packet of frozen mice.

Gengus preferred the fresh variety, but so long as they were not rock hard, he would eat them slowly and methodically. The packet of mice had been left thawing in the sink in some warm water. If they were still too hard Jeff would zap them in the microwave. He was about to unwrap the packet of mice when the phone rang. It was the now retired DCI Susan Parker calling from Bayfield.

"Jeff Whitaker speaking."

Susan told him about the strange note that she'd found and asked to meet up with him.

Jeff looked at his watch. He had scheduled to meet up with his team in Clinton at the OPP headquarters where they had promised he could set up an incident room, but that wasn't until tomorrow. He didn't particularly want to drive all the way back to Bayfield again.

" Could I call in and pick up the note early tomorrow morning, I'm in London right now."

"Yes, sure, what time should I expect you?"

Jeff thought for a minute. He had asked his team to be in Clinton for nine a.m. "How about eight-fifteen a.m.?"

 Susan coughed and thought, there goes my lie-in, but answered Jeff politely. "Yes, that would be fine. See you then tomorrow."

Jeff put the phone down. He had got to know both Rose Blair and Susan Parker the previous year after the murder at the winery, but he felt that both their reputations for solving countless murders in and around Bayfield was impressive.

Their involvement could also however, hinder a murder investigation and thus could be, a big pain in the neck. C'est la vie, Jeff thought, if they helped him to find the murderer it would in turn help his team as long as both women didn't get in the way.

Right now, they had very little to go on. Nobody at the White Squirrel had seen a dicky bird. The assassin must have been very good not leaving a single trace of his whereabouts. This note left for Susan had added an unexpected twist, one that indeed might be the undoing of the murderer.

EIGHT

Susan left Rose and Tom's house feeling decidedly unsettled. Ian wouldn't be home for at least three hours, and she was reluctant to go back to her empty house. Of course, she knew that she was being irrational, but the thought that the perpetrator knew where she lived made her feel nervous. She decided to go for a walk on the beach. Leaving Rose and Tom's house she drove her silver Porsche down to Pioneer Park where she parked and got out.

What a beautiful day, Susan thought, not too hot, but warm enough to go out without a jacket. Susan was still in her golfing attire. She hadn't had time to change, but at least she was dressed for the sun.

Walking down the wooden steps to the sandy beach below the park she let out a deep sigh. What a day, she thought, I could do without this just before my wedding. She sighed again and then Susan kicked off her shoes, rolled up her capris and waded into the lovely water. It was icy cold. She jumped back and almost fell over in the rush to get out of the water.

Susan continued to walk along the beach until she reached the long pier and the car park. She rolled down her capris and slipped her shoes back on and preceded to walk up the hill towards the Mara St. Walkway. This would take her back up to Pioneer Park and to where she had left her car.

Going for a walk had given her time to reflect and put everything into perspective. She would drive home and cook a nice meal for Ian and put the weird note out of her mind. After all, if the saying was in effect "tit for tat"' then, in theory, everything was now even.

Of course, it would help if she could identify the person that she or her team had supposedly killed in the line of duty to warrant the death of her niece Mary. It had been over five years since that whole drug cartel bust and, of course, she had been in an emotional roller-coaster ride then with the start of her relationship with Tonne, the drug-squad officer. So much water under the bridge, and now she was about to tie the knot again with Ian and she wasn't at all sure what she felt. Sure, she loved Ian, but was he the right man for her? Tonne had been passionate and there had never been a dull moment with him, but he was also impetuous and a drug user, not to mention a gambler, whereas Ian was steady and calm, her solid rock, reliable and safe.

Susan had reached Bayfield Terrace and could see her silver Porsche parked by the roadside. It was time to get a grip and stop thinking so much.

NINE

DCI Jeff Whitaker arrived at the OPP headquarters in Clinton a good twenty minutes before his team. The Chief Superintendent had popped into the incident room and asked if everything was set up as he wanted. Jeff had looked around the light and airy room, noting the large white board against the wall and the big conference table with ten chairs as well as a big screen smart T.V.

"Everything looks shipshape to me. Did you manage to secure the team I requested?"

The chief smiled, "Yes, they all jumped at the opportunity to work on a murder case. Not many of those in Huron County these days."

Jeff was about to dispute this fact when Constable Maya Patel breezed into the room. A huge smile alighted her face when she saw Jeff. Maya had worked the previous year with

DCI Whittaker helping to solve the murder at the winery.

Although only in her twenties she had proved invaluable with her computer skills and was a greatly respected and popular member of the whole team

"DCI Whitaker, great to be working with you again."

She took a seat at the table and opened her laptop ready for their meeting. Sergeant Jennings was next to arrive. He nodded to Maya and Jeff and took his seat.

The chief smiled at them all and ducked out of the room leaving Jeff to marshal his thoughts. Ten minutes later Constables Brown and Elliott sauntered in and, seeing everyone obviously waiting for them, they skulked into their seats looking suitably abashed. They were only five minutes late; the others had arrived ten minutes early.

Jeff decided to get the ball rolling." Welcome everyone and can I say how pleased I am to be working with you all again. Now, this is a slightly unusual case, hopefully we'll know more when forensics get back to us, but this is what we do know. Yesterday this young woman was shot at The White Squirrel golf course."

Jeff produced a photograph and using a small circular magnetic disk he attached it to the whiteboard.

"Mary Malloy, age 43, resident of 52 Kensington Drive, Exeter. She was playing golf with her friend Jane and at 11:05 was shot with a rifle. We will know more when the bullet is extracted. Neither Jane nor any of the other golfers interviewed witnessed the actual shooter. From the trajectory of the fatal bullet taken from the body the forensic officers calculated approximately where the assassin took his shot.

A clump of trees located some four hundred metres away from the tee appears the likely spot. I'm still waiting for the final forensic report from the IDENT unit.

Now an interesting twist to this case is that the deceased, Mary Malloy, is the niece of recently retired DCI Susan Parker who was coincidently also playing golf in the women's league at the White Squirrel Golf course when the murder took place.

An additional twist has also arisen in the form of a note dropped off at Susan Parker's condo yesterday. and which may or may not be connected to this case."

Jeff passed the note around for his team to look at." As you can see it is a biblical reference from the Book of Exodus. Basically, it is the old saying about an eye for an eye and a tooth for a tooth.

Quite how this ties in with a murder we don't know yet, but it does seem to be too much of a coincidence that this note was delivered to her house on the same day as the murder of her niece"

He paused while the team all had time to read the note.

" Any thoughts?"

There was complete silence in the room, Constable Patel started to click on her computer pulling up the biblical reference in full. She read it out to everyone and then said, "It's obviously all about retribution and reciprocation Sir. Miss Parker must have royally pissed someone off."

"Anymore thoughts?"

Still more silence in the room until PC Elliot spoke up hesitantly at first. "The victim had been part of the Mennonite community hadn't she, Sir?

Jeff nodded his head

"Yes, she left the order about four years ago and moved to Exeter. Where are you going with this Constable?"

"Well, about four years ago we had a spot of trouble with the Mennonites and I'm sure that Ms. Parker was the DCI in charge of the case then. Maybe there is a connection, the victim might have been still part of the community then, I just don't know. It's just a thought."

"And a damn good thought too, Constable. Right, I'm going to put you and Constable Brown on to exploring the Mennonite connection. Sergeant Jennings, I'd like you to set up a team interviewing the public to see if we can identify any vehicles or persons of interest that may have been seen in the vicinity of the residences of Mary Malloy and of Susan Parker as well as around the golf course.

Start off with interviewing Mary Malloy's friends and neighbors in Exeter and then extend it to the houses on highway 21 overlooking the White Squirrel Golf Course. We should probably also interview the neighbours at Susan Parker's condo in Bayfield and maybe the restaurants in Bayfield.

Constable Patel, you're coming with me. We have an autopsy to attend to in Goderich."

"On your motorbike, Sir?" Maya asked a little nervously.

"No, no, I'll come with you in your car, if you don't mind, unless you want to ride pillion with me?"

"OK, everyone, we will meet back here tomorrow and hopefully we'll have something to put on this rather empty whiteboard by then."

There was a shuffling of feet and a few murmurs of "See you, sir", and then the room was empty, and DCI Whitaker was left following Constable Patel out to the rear car park. A bright yellow beetle Volkswagen was parked incongruously between two OPP cruisers.

"Here you are, Sir, this is Bessie, my beetle."

"Bessie?"

"Yes, Sir, I always name my cars. My last car was called Goldie, that was really a no brainer as it was a gold-coloured car and the one before that was Ruby......."

Jeff interrupted her, boy could she talk he thought to himself. "Yes, well, we better be going as Dr. Green will be waiting to start the autopsy."

Fifteen minutes later they were parked outside the pathology department. DCI Whitaker felt quite faint. Not only had his Constable not stopped talking, but she drove like a maniac on speed.

They entered the clinical building and were immediately greeted with the smell of formaldehyde and disinfectant. Constable Patel wrinkled her nose and said out loud. "I hate mortuaries. Do I really have to go inside?"

"Yes, Constable, the law requires us to be witness to the autopsy. Don't worry, Dr Green is normally quite quick and efficient. We will be in and out within the hour."

Soon they were ushered into a gloomy, white tiled room with a whole wall installed with stainless steel pullouts. 'Christ, how many bodies do they have stored in here?' Jeff thought to himself. His reverie was interrupted by Dr Green who appeared as if from thin air. He was a tall man wearing surgical scrubs, a little surgical cap and a mask adorning his face. Only his eyes came to view, and they showed warmth and kindness.

"So, DCI Whittaker, who have we got here?"

He approached Maya and put out his hand. "Doctor Green but call me doc or Ian".

Maya smiled, "Constable Patel, but you can call me Maya". They both laughed and with that the ice was broken.

"Right, well let's get on with it.'

Ian pulled a gurney over to the wall of stainless-steel drawers and pulled out the one nearest the door. Mary Malloy was laid out on the steel slab. Ian adjusted his microphone head set and his laptop computer. Turning to Jeff and Maya he said, "Right, here I go." He picked up a shiny silver scalpel and preceded to make a large Y shaped incision across the front of Mary's body.

Constable Maya, almost as if she was in slow motion, crumpled in a dead faint.

"Is this her first time" Ian said as Jeff, having caught her before she hit the floor, helped her stand upright and walk over to the single chair which sat by the entrance to the Mortuary.

"I think that she can sit this one out, don't you?" Jeff said and returned to the slab where Ian had already pulled out the bullet. He plopped the bloodied shell into an evidence bag and sealed and dated it and then put his whole hand into the cavity and removed the heart and then the liver. Each was examined and then weighed and dropped into a bowl and so it went on for another twenty minutes until all the vital organs had been similarly examined, weighed and then returned to the body. Finally, the cavity was sewn up and Jeff and Maya were able to escape.

"Do you fancy a coffee" Jeff asked a still pale looking Maya.

"Oh, yes, please."

They headed out of Goderich back to Clinton on highway 8 until reaching Cait's Cafe where they pulled over and went inside. Five minutes later they were seated by the window sipping a large latte.

"Doctor Green has promised to get his report to us by tomorrow" Jeff said in between gulps of milky coffee.

Maya was quiet, she still felt awkward after fainting in the morgue.

"You know something, Constable, if you gave me a dollar for everyone who's fainted in the morgue, I'd be a rich man now. Don't beat yourself up, honestly, it's not worth it."

She smiled wanly.

"Right, when you're finished you can drop me off in Clinton and then you can go home. We'll call it a day."

TEN

Susan had spent the morning thinking about her niece Mary. She felt so sad when she remembered the fresh young face that had greeted Rose and her so exuberantly the previous day. Why had they not kept in touch, she thought. There was something from Mary's past that was niggling her and she wasn't quite sure what it was? Her niece's life hadn't been easy that was clear, particularly during her years with the Mennonites, but she had appeared happy yesterday. Once again Susan regretted not keeping in touch with Mary. There really had been no excuse as Exeter was just down the road. Admittedly it was a two- way street, Mary had not reached out to Susan either, but then neither of them knew where the other lived, which was ironic as they were practically neighbours.

The telephone rang and broke Susan's reverie. It was her fiancé, Ian.

"How are you doing love? I know this must be hard for you. Look, I've just finished the autopsy and after I've written up my notes I'm going to head home early. Do you fancy going out for dinner tonight?"

"Oh, that would be great, Ian. See you soon."

She'd really lucked out when she had met Ian, Susan thought, although theirs had been a slow, simmering, relationship built upon friendship and the more gruesome connection of pathology.

They had first met over five years ago when she'd been investigating the murders at the Little Inn. Ian had, in fact, taken her out for a drink at the Black Dog, but then she had met Tony and had fallen in love with the drug squad officer.

They had both left the police force and gone off to live in Italy together, which was super romantic to begin with until Susan discovered that Tony not only had a problem with alcohol, but he also owed money to a lot of not very nice people. She had left him when it became obvious that he'd become involved in the underworld of drugs and organised crime.

Since breaking up with Tony, Susan had returned to Bayfield and had been immediately snatched up again by the Serious Crimes unit. It was while investigating the murder of Juliet Carmichael that Ian and she had got together again and become romantically involved.

At the memory of the retreat murder, Susan sat up abruptly, knocking her sleepy cat off her lap in her startled haste to stand up. The Juliet Carmichael case had a Mennonite connection. Could the killing of her niece have anything to do with that old case? It was Mary's Mennonite connection that had alerted Susan. Just how much did Mary know about the drug trafficking that took place within the community?

She'd left the community four years ago. How long ago was the drug bust now, maybe five years, she would have to check. If, and it was a huge, if, her niece had somehow been involved, could that be motivation for murder? But why five years after the event?

ELEVEN

Rose, too, had been dwelling on the case and had come to almost the same conclusion as Susan; the Mennonite connection seemed the only thing that possibly made any sense. An eye for an eye, a tooth for tooth, real Old Testament dogma expressing the principle of retribution which seemed so old hat in modern day parlance.

Remembering how desperate Tom and she had felt when they had been abducted and tied up in the pig barn by that awful man Hank Wiebe and his wife. How could she ever forget how scared they both had felt. Sonia and James Anderson came to mind, they were pig farmers too, but were they also Mennonites?

If she remembered correctly there had been several Mennonite farms involved in the drug trafficking in and around the Elora area in Wellington County. But who had been killed? The only victim that came to mind was the unfortunate Juliette Carmichael, who was not a Mennonite herself, but was dealing in drugs. Just what was the connection? For the life of her Rose just couldn't see.

Just then the telephone rang. Looking at the screen Rose saw that it was Jessica calling presumably from Montreal. She answered the call straight away.

"Hi Jessica darling, is everything alright?"

There was a slight pause before Jessica answered." Well, mom, no, everything is not alright. We've got a real problem with Abby. She refuses to go to school and I'm at my wits end. I can't force her to go, Rob and I have tried reasoning with her, and I spoke to her teacher, and she doesn't understand what the problem is either. Perhaps if you spoke to her, she might reveal the real issue?

Rose adored her two granddaughters Abby and Lily. They came and stayed with Tom and her every summer for a week or two and they always had such a good time together. Normally Abby was a happy child although since she had turned thirteen, she had become more reserved and rather sullen. That was a terrible age thought Rose, just the beginning of adolescence and going into grade eight where the atmosphere was laden with male testosterone and the girls were bitchy and moody. Poor Abby, Rose thought. She strongly suspected that bullying might be at the root of the problem.

"Oh, darling, of course I'll speak to her. Is she there right now?"

In answer to her question, she heard Abbey pick up the phone. "Hi grandma."

"Hi darling. Your mom just told me that you're having some problems at school. Do you want to tell me about it, love?"

There was a moment of silence down the line and then Abbey spoke softly. "Melissa posted a picture of me in my bikini on Instagram. She took the picture last summer when we were at the swimming pool. I didn't even know she'd taken it and now all the boys are making mean comments about me and I'm so embarrassed. I want to hide"

Abby's voice started to quiver, and Roses heart gave a lurch. Cyberbullying was a real concern. She had read of cases where kids had committed suicide over similar postings.

"Oh, my darling, that's awful. Did you tell your teachers?"

Abby sniffed loudly.

"No, grandma, if I did it would only make things worse. Oh, I hate school so much"

"Listen darling, you only have a couple of weeks left until the summer holidays and then you start high school in September. Just hold on for a few more weeks and all will be OK."

"Oh, I can't go back to school grandma, I really can't. I hate Melissa."

Abby started to sob out loud. Jessica took the phone from her daughter and said, "Well, at least you got to the root of the problem mom. I can understand why she feels so hopeless."

Rose answered seriously. "You know, Jessica, you could always bring her down here for the last two weeks of school. Her teacher would understand and being away from Montreal might help her. Your father and I would love to have her stay with us."

There was silence down the line and then Jessica sighed deeply. "That's so good of you, mom. Let me talk it over with Rob and Abby. It would mean that she'll miss out on all the end of year celebrations, but I don't think that will matter and she's finished this year's curricula. I'll call you back later."

Rose put the phone down and stood in the kitchen quietly thinking how mean teenage girls could be. Tom walked in from the garden and looked at his wife with a worried frown on his face.

"Everything alright, love?"

"No, it isn't, Tom."

She preceded to tell him all about Abby and the cyber bullying.

"Poor mite." Tom said.

Before Rose could say anything else the telephone rang again. Rose picked it up straight away and rather curtly answered,

"Rose Blair speaking."

"Oh, mom, you sound really pissed off. Is anything the matter?"

It was Anne, Tom and Rose's other daughter who lived in Toronto. Anne had separated from her husband, Greg several years ago and they currently shared custody of their two children Oliver and Amelia.

Greg lived in the same condo building as Anne which made sharing the children very easy. Greg had subsequently met a woman, Merrill, who had moved in with him. Fortunately, Merril adored Amelia and Olver and everything appeared to be working out okay. Anne had since gone through several relationships mostly through an online dating app. So far though, there had been no-one serious until she met Scott who she had been dating now for over six months.

'Anne, lovely to hear you. Sorry, love, I was just feeling angry about poor Abby and the cyber bullying going on in her school."

Rose proceeded to tell Anne all about the incident.

"Oh, mom, that sounds awful. Poor Abby. Do you think she's going to be okay staying with you for a few weeks?"

"Oh yes, she'll be fine. I've got lots for her do to keep her distracted from the mean kids in her school. Anyhow, darling, how are you and the kids?"

There was a pause the other end of the line, and then Anne let out a deep sigh,

"Well mom, Scott and I have split up. He couldn't take the next step which was to move in with me. He was frightened of the commitment."

There was a little sob which Anne covered up with a cough.

"But I didn't phone you to moan about my love life. Honestly, I'm through with men. What I wanted to check with you was are the kids registered for the Celtic Camp? I know last year you put their names down round about this time. They do so love going to the camp. It's fabulous."

"Yes, darling, we registered them last month so no worries on that front. I do have to say though, that your father and I really liked Scott. Are you sure you can't figure it out and still stay together?"

"I wish we could, mom, but he made it clear that he never wanted to be a father, and he would in effect be that to Amelia and Oliver, if they moved in with each other."

Rose thought that couples made it so difficult for themselves and surely if they loved each other, they could make it work. But obviously there lay the answer, they didn't love each other enough to make it work. She let out a deep sigh.

"Well, I'm so sorry to hear that and I know it will take time to process your feelings and move on with your life. Anyway, are you coming down to visit us soon? I'm sure Abby would love to see her cousins again."

"Yes, I'll try to get down in the next couple of weeks. Okay mom, I must go, work calls."

Rose put her phone away and frowned. "Oh, Tom, the world is not a kind place, is it?"

Tom looked at his wife fondly and said, "No it isn't, love, but as long as we keep being kind ourselves then we'll be doing our bit for mankind, hey!"

TWELVE

Ian drove home in silence. Normally he liked to listen to the radio and chill out after a day's work, but the autopsy of the young woman, Mary, had disturbed his normally calm mind. What a waste of a young life, he thought and then he countered that with the fact that at least her death was instant. She wouldn't have had time to register pain or even surprise. Whoever had pulled the trigger had certainly known what they were doing, Ian thought, it had been a clean and instantly fatal shot. The killer knew exactly what he or she was doing, Ian thought, and he would put money on the shooter being a trained marksperson. But still, a professional hit on a young woman seemed unlikely and it was this thought that was playing on Ian's mind.

When he arrived at the condo he tripped over the front step and if it hadn't been for Susan opening the door and breaking his fall, he would have ended up flat on his face and maybe injured himself.

"Whoa... steady there, Ian." Susan said as she helped him regain a standing position.

"Are you alright?"

Ian laughed and kissed Susan as he stepped inside the condo.

"Yes, I'm fine darling, just a little preoccupied that's all. I'm just going to hop in the shower before we go out to dinner. I thought we could go to The Black Dog and then maybe wander down to The Little Inn for a drink afterwards. We need to check in with them to see if everything is on track with the wedding arrangements."

Susan grinned. Ian was more excited about their impending wedding than she was. Whilst this would be her third time around, for Ian marrying Susan would be his first and hopefully his last wedding.

They had chosen The Little Inn for their wedding venue as they were just going to have a small gathering of about 40 guests and the inn could accommodate that number perfectly. The wedding service and reception would both take place in the same area.

Twenty minutes later Susan and Ian pulled up outside the Black Dog. It was a beautiful evening with just a soft, gentle summer breeze rippling through the leaves on the trees down Main Street.

"Should we sit inside or outside?" Ian asked.

Susan hated being either too hot or too cold when eating outdoors. She opted for dining inside. As they entered the restaurant Andrew, the barman, waved them over. They wandered up to the bar. It was obvious that Andrew wanted to talk to them.

"Hi Susan, Ian, you're here for dinner, are you?"

 "Yes, but we'll have a drink first." Ian said as they both took stools at the bar.

"So...". Andrew began, "I heard that a young woman was shot at the White Squirrel today. Do you know anything about it?"

Susan nodded. She was reluctant to talk about her niece's murder, but she also knew that the gossip in the village would be rampant. Somehow the locals always seemed to get the scoop before even the police.

"You know a strange man was in here not too long after the shooting." Andrew said as he poured out two beers for Susan and Ian.

"In what way was he strange and why would you think that he was connected to the shooting?" Susan said.

"I'm not sure why I think he's connected, I suppose it's just the timing, but it was his accent and his reticence. It was almost as if he didn't want to be heard."

"So, what accent did he have?" Susan asked while sipping her ice- cold beer.

"Well, at first, I thought he was Australian, and then South African or maybe Rhodesian. They all sound alike to me."

"What did he look like?" Susan asked putting down her drink and pulling out her notebook.

"He was about your height, Ian, but swarthy in complexion as if he worked outdoors a lot. Dark brown curly hair; looked as if he was pretty fit, very muscular in build, but it was his eyes that caught my attention. They were an unusual green speckled with yellow, reminded me of leopard's eyes."

"Have you told the police any of this, Andy?" Susan asked.

"Well, actually the police were here this afternoon asking questions, but it wasn't my shift then."

"You do need to give them the details of the man you just described. It could be totally unrelated to the inquiry, but on the other hand, it might prove to be a vital piece of evidence."

"OK, I'll contact the police. They left a contact number. Anything I can do to help catch the culprit."

Leopard eyes, Susan thought, where have I heard that description before and in what context?

THIRTEEN

PC Elliot arrived first, carrying a tray of coffee and a box of doughnuts precariously balanced on top of each other. He whistled a tuneless tune as he entered the building, looking around eagerly for the rest of the team.

There was no sign of anyone, but he was early and so he walked down to the incident room and plonked down the coffee and donuts and stood there looking at the white board which now sported a large picture of Mary Malloy and not much else.

Hopefully the team would gather some vital information that might pad out the rather empty board. He had just sat down and was about to choose his favorite doughnut, the Boston cream, when Constable Maya burst into the room.

"Hiya", she said, "Are these for everyone?"

"Sure, help yourself, the treats are on me." PC Elliot said as he bit into his donut. "How was the autopsy?"

Maya put her coffee down and said grimly, "Enough said on that the better, but I survived the ordeal."

PC Elliott pulled a face, "Sorry to say, but it never gets easier, although I suppose you get a bit hardened to it after awhile."

Voices could be heard down the hallway and soon the room was bustling, but DCI Whitaker still hadn't arrived. Just as they were wondering if they should start the meeting without him PC Elliot received a text message saying that the DCI had been unavoidably detained and would be about 15 minutes late. Could he start the meeting.

In truth, DCI Whitaker had spent a whole hour trying to find Gengus. He'd woken up as usual that morning, made his morning cup of tea and was in the middle of getting his breakfast when he realized that Gengus had not appeared. Normally the two of them would eat breakfast together, Gengus munching on a couple of dead mice, while he ate his crunchy toast.

So, where was his scaly pet? Eventually, after looking everywhere, he was found sound asleep in the bottom of the wastebasket beside the toilet in the bathroom. DCI Whitaker was so relieved that he had given Gengus an extra mouse and then had made great haste to leave his apartment. Jumping on his bike he had driven to Clinton as fast as he could for his team meeting.

PC Elliot was in full swing when DCI Whitaker blustered into the room. He stopped mid-sentence and welcomed the DCI.

"Sir, I was just saying that forensics have sent their finding's, and it makes for interesting reading. Oh, and Doctor Green has also forwarded his pathologist report. Here you are sir."

DCI Whitaker scanned the computer print out before reading it to his team, concluding with,

"So, it looks like our victim was killed by a single bullet shot from a Tikka T3 light rifle. A clean professional shot, instant death as we had deducted ourselves. It looks like Mary was a mother, her uterus had given birth to at least one child. Apart from that, she was otherwise a healthy woman still in her prime.

Right let's have your reports. PC Elliot and PC Brown, you were looking into the Mennonite connection. What if anything, did you find out?"

 PC Elliott and PC Brown shuffled some papers around and then PC Elliott stood up and began to speak.

"Mary Malloy left the Mennonite community up in Listowel four years ago. Nobody was prepared to talk about why she left, and I couldn't find her husband or for that matter her son to speak to. It was as if the whole community shut down when I mentioned her name. Her son, Joshia is, we believe about fourteen years old, and he works with his father making furniture, particularly chairs. They live in a farmhouse two kilometres north of Listowel, coincidentally their farm is located adjacent to the Anderson's pig farm."

DCI Whittaker looked at them blankly, "What pray, is significant about the Anderson farm?"

PC Elliot looked at PC Brown meaningfully and then continued saying, "About six years ago, sir, there was a big drug bust. Cocaine from Mexico and Venezuela was being moved across southern Ontario using Mennonite farms as their drops. Most of those farms were dotted around Listowel, Milverton, Milbank and Elora.

The Anderson farm was the scene of an abduction where Rose and Tom Blair were kidnapped and rescued by one of the undercover drug squad team. It was all in the news. There were several people killed and the whole drug bust put a stop to the cartel. The whole thing featured on prime television on the 5th Estate."

"Okay, so who was killed and is there any connection to our Mary Malloy?" DCI Whittaker asked.

PC Elliot looked down at his notes before replying.

"Juliet Carmichael, James Anderson and Seb Miller were all murdered by Isabelle Cabella, the great granddaughter of President Diosdado, shadow chief of the drug cartel known as the Cartel of the Sun.

Lydia Klassen is currently serving time but will be ready for parole this year. Isabelle was extradited back to Venezuela. Lydia Klassen is Francis Klassen's niece, and he was the one caught smuggling cocaine into Canada from

Mexico. From what I've gathered, Francis took his own life while in prison. We haven't found any direct connection to Mary Malloy other than the fact that she was a Mennonite living on a farm near where the drug bust took place."

DCI Whittaker nodded and thanked the constables. "Now Sergeant Jennings, how did you get on with interviewing the public?"

Sergeant Jennings gathered up his notes and glanced at his laptop.

"Well, not much luck with the Exeter bunch. Jane, Mary's golfing friend, could barely talk as she was so upset. She had known Mary since Kindergarten, although had lost touch with her when she moved to Listowel and joined the Mennonite community.

Neighbours said that Mary had kept herself to herself and had nothing further to add. However, we did speak to most of the shopkeepers on Main Street in Bayfield and a couple of the retailers reckoned that they saw a beefy looking man parked in front of The Black Dog. We asked the bar keeper, but he wasn't working that day. He suggested that we come back this afternoon and speak to Andrew who was apparently on duty the day of the murder."

Just then as if in answer to DC Jennings, his cell phone rang. Looking at the screen he shouted, 'bingo'. It was Andrew from The Black Dog reaching out to him with information about the beefy looking man with an Australian/ South African accent.

DC Jennings put his phone away and smiled as he recalled Andrew and his description of the man.

"Did he see what car he was driving?" DCI Whittaker asked.

Sergeant Jennings looked at his notes again and said,

" No. The man just quietly left the bar without saying a single word. Nobody I spoke to saw the car he drove away in."

"Thank you, Sergeant." DCI Whitaker turned to his team and said, "So, what have we learned? Not a lot I'm afraid, although I'm sure Mary's connection to the Mennonites is somehow related to this case.

Constable Elliot, can you do a deep search into Isabelle Carella, the great granddaughter of the head of the cartel.

Where is she now? If she was extradited back to Venezuela does that mean she's free or is she still incarcerated somewhere? If Mary was somehow involved with the drug cartel, why has it taken six years for anything to have happened? I want answers team, so dig deep and let's find out more about the drugs and the Mennonites."

There was a general murmur amongst the team. DCI Whitaker started to collect up his papers and was about to leave when Constable Patel spoke up.

"Sir, do we know anything about the child Mary had and how old is he or she?"

DCI Whitaker looked up and directly at Maya.

"Right, Constable, I charge you with finding everything, and I say everything, about Mary's family. OK? Right, we'll meet back here the same time tomorrow. Let's get some answers."

The team traipsed out of the incident room followed by a very dispirited DCI Whitaker

FOURTEEN

Susan slept in late. By the time she woke up, Ian had already left for work, and it was just her and Fluffy who was curled up on her bed gently snoring away. She got up and showered and then went down to the kitchen to make a pot of coffee. She was just buttering some toast when there was a knock on her front door. Looking out of the window Susan could see a very agitated Jane standing on the doorstep. She went to the door and let her in

"Oh, hi Jane. Come in. I've just made some coffee. Come and join me. In fact, let's go out onto the patio, it's such a beautiful morning."

Jane followed Susan out onto the patio where her hot tub took pride of place. Seeing Jane looking at the beast Susan laughed, "It was my retirement present to myself. Yes, I know it's huge and it does take up most of the patio space, but I love it."

Jane smiled." Your niece Mary talked about getting a hot tub too."

Susan took Jane's hand and gently said, "Tell me about her, Jane. I feel that I barely knew anything about my own niece."

Jane let out a deep sigh and opened her purse. Putting her hand in she pulled out an envelope and handed it over to Susan.

"Mary made me promise to give you this in the event of her death."

Susan took the envelope and turned it over in her hands. It was addressed to DCI Parker.

"So how did you find my address, Jane?" Susan asked.

"Oh, I asked around and I know what you're going to say next. Yes, Mary did know that you lived in Bayfield. She often talked about her clever aunt who was a detective."

Susan still looked puzzled.

"But why didn't she contact me? I never even knew she was living in Exeter."

Jane's face looked conflicted. She paused before answering.

"There is much you don't know about Mary. Did you know that she was hiding from the

Mennonites? That her husband and son refused to help her, that she hadn't got a bean to her name when she came knocking on my door four years ago?"

Jane's eyes began to well-up as she quietly continued.

"It's my fault that she was killed. You see she was like a frightened mouse when she first came to Exeter, wouldn't leave my house, was terrified that she would be found by Samuel. Over the last year I gave her a false sense of security, encouraged her to leave the house and to even play golf. If I hadn't had done that, she would still be alive."

Jane started to cry, and Susan went over and put her arms around her shaking shoulders.

"Don't blame yourself, Jane. Believe me, whoever killed Mary would have got her one way or another, but I still don't understand why she didn't reach out to me for help."

Jane shook her head.

"I'm not sure why she didn't contact you either. Maybe the letter might explain."

Susan looked at the envelope again. She was reluctant to open it while Jane was there.

"Right, let's have our coffee and then we'll talk some more."

FIFTEEN

Jessica had texted her mother to say that they would be bringing Abby down at the weekend and that she was really looking forward to her stay at grandma and grandpas. Rose read the message and smiled. Calling out to Tom that breakfast was ready she preceded to pour out the coffee. It was boiled eggs today and she was reluctant to put them on until Tom had appeared. He always spent a long time getting up in the mornings and Rose had learned to be patient when waiting for him. She busied herself with making some toast and putting out the butter and marmalade.

Today it was her turn to man the tasting room at Huron Estates Winery. She had to be there by eleven to open the tasting room and would be in attendance until three in the afternoon. Typically, she was kept busy enough, but it was always nicer if Tom or Susan could be there with her. Tom was working on his boat this morning so he wouldn't be available to keep her company, but maybe Susan would be free? She picked up her phone and called Susan.

"Susan speaking."

"Oh, great, you're in. Any chance of you joining me at the tasting room today? I'm on duty from eleven until three and I would love your company."

Susan didn't reply straight away, but then she said,

"I've just had Jane, Mary's friend here this morning. She gave me a letter from Mary to be read in the event of her death. To be honest I'm a bit shocked, Rose. Yes, I'll come and help you, if you help me out with Mary's letter. It's left me feeling somewhat conflicted."

"It all sounds intriguing and yes, of course you can sound me out. We'll have a good chinwag over a glass of wine and if it's quiet enough I'll make us a charcuterie board for our lunch. So, I'll see you there sometime after eleven."

Rose put the phone down just as Tom appeared in the kitchen. She turned the saucepan on containing the eggs and waited patiently for the water to boil. Five minutes later they were eating their boiled eggs and reviewing the day ahead.

"The starter motor on Tranquility is still playing up." Tom said in between a mouthful of toast.

"Do you think that you need a new motor then?" Rose asked.

 Tom shook his head.

"Well, I put a new one in last year so it should be OK."

"Didn't you say that water had leaked in from somewhere over the winter? Maybe it's rusted up the engine?"

Rose knew very little about engines, but she did know that rust could cause all sorts of problems.

"You could be right, love. I'll see when I open it up this morning. Did I hear you arranging to meet up with Susan at the tasting room today?"

"Yes, she's got some information about her niece she wants to talk about. I'll tell you all about it when I get back."

Tom took old Ben out for a quick walk before heading down to the Marina. Rose cleared the breakfast stuff away and generally did a quick tidy up. She then changed into what she called her work clothes, a smart crimson silk top with co-ordinating pants, got into her car and drove to the winery.

There was no sign of Renee and Rose's old Volvo was currently the sole vehicle in the otherwise deserted parking lot. Ashton, was however, out in the vineyard on the tractor cutting grass. He had been taken on at the beginning of the summer as a vineyard helper and had proved a godsend.

SIXTEEN

Rose unlocked the big doors to the tasting room. She then gathered together the outside umbrellas and set them up in the rear patio area.   Next, she went into the small kitchen and pulled out one of the large blocks of cheese and preceded to dice it up into neat little cubes. Filling several small baskets with assorted crackers, she carried them through to the tasting room countertop.

Looking at her watch Rose decided to carry out the open sign and place it on the side of the road by the winery entrance. She was just walking back to the building when Susan pulled up in her gleaming silver Porsche. Rose watched her glamorous friend get out of her car with admiration. She was wearing beige pants and a cream linen blouse. A bright turquoise scarf was tied around her neck and her shoulder length auburn hair glistened in the sunshine.

"Hi, Rose." Susan said as she walked over to Rose "Let's hope it's a quiet day as I've got loads to tell you."

Walking into the winery, Susan and Rose went over to the bar and started setting out the tasting racks.

After awhile Rose said,

"OK, Susan, spill the beans, what have you learned about your mysterious niece?"

Susan put down the glasses she'd been polishing and spoke.

"Well, she certainly led a strange life. Look it might be better if you read this letter she left for me."

Susan fished about in her bag, pulled out an envelope addressed to DCI Parker and handed the letter to Rose who opened it straight away.

Dear Susan,

If you are reading this, it will mean that I am dead. You will be asking all manner of questions and hopefully I'll be able to set your mind straight on what has led to my demise. I do remember you, dear aunt, as being very clever and I hope that you might be able to find justice for my death. You see Susan, I have been a despicable liar and a thief and if I was to believe the dogma of the Mennonites, I will have got what I deserved. But nobody deserves to have been treated like an entity, to be a slave and a chattel for every man in the community. I rebelled against all of this and managed to break free, but I will always be punished for my behavior. You know, I truly loved Samuel when we were first together, and I ran away to be with him and joined his community of Mennonites. I was young and totally in love and wanted to embrace all that was Samuel, and I did so wholeheartedly for the first four years.

A year after I was married, Joshua was born, and I threw myself into motherhood and couldn't have been happier. I had my little family that I worshipped and adored and then there were whispers amongst the Elders that I was about ready for my initiation. Susan, I never knew that I was to be shared with the other men in the community and, if I refused, I would be beaten and locked away until submission. There followed a time in my life that I wish to forget, the only saving grace was my little boy, Joshua. He was still too young to understand what the men in the community wanted from the women. It was during this period that I became aware that my husband Samuel was involved in the trafficking of drugs.

I learned that this involved a large Mexican and Venezuelan drug Cartel, and the Mennonite farmers were being used as mules to transport and hide vast quantities of cocaine. Nobody knew that I had discovered a cache of emeralds which were delivered along with the cocaine to Samuel. His job was to sell the emeralds to a jeweler in London and pay the farmers with the cash from the sale of the jewels. Over a period of years, I took handfuls of emeralds out of the stash deposited with Samuel. I reasoned that nobody would be any wiser and it would be my nest egg should I ever be able to leave the community. You see Susan, I had nothing. No bank account, no money, no phone, just the clothes on my back.

Joshua was about ten when I felt that I had accumulated enough emeralds, this was just after the drug bust when several Mennonite farmers were arrested. Fortunately, Samuel had only dealt with the emeralds, so no cocaine was ever found on our farm. The Anderson's across the way were busted and the Klassens. I believe there were some deaths involved too.

I had planned my escape carefully. Once a week Samuel, Joshua and I went into Listowel to shop. If I could only get away from Samuel long enough to not be seen walking away, then I would stand a chance of hitching a ride with someone. I didn't care where to so long as it was miles away from Listowel and the Mennonite community. I would of course take Joshua with me. But what I hadn't accounted for was Joshua's closeness and loyalty to his father. On that fateful day, everything went as I had planned. Samuel left Josh and I in the supermarket while he went down the road to the hardware store to shop. This was very much my cue to escape. I grabbed Joshua's hand and ran out of the shop looking along the road at the parked cars until I saw a nice-looking couple about to drive off in their car. I rushed up to them and asked if they could give my son and myself a ride and they smiled and said "Hop-in". It was then that Samuel appeared and seeing what was happening he called out to Joshua who let go of my hand and ran to his father. I had a choice, to escape with the couple and forfeit my son, or to stay. I chose to escape. Please don't judge me too harshly. I knew that Joshua would be well looked after by the community, he was already showing signs of maturity and a liking for the way of life afforded to the Mennonite male. In my heart I knew that I would never survive if I stayed any longer. So, with a heavy heart I went off with the nice couple who were heading for Sarnia. I had nothing with me but my purse which contained thousands of dollars worth of emeralds. I have been living off those emeralds ever since.

So that is my story and if I'm dead I would suspect my husband Samuel or any one of the Elders of the community as being responsible for my demise. If you find Samuel and Joshua, please tell them that I forgive them and I will always love them.

So sorry to burden you with this, Aunty Susan. The key in the envelope is for a bank safe deposit box at the RBC bank in Exeter.

You will find what remains of the emeralds in a bag there. I have notified the bank that you have power of attorney and therefore are the only one with access to the box. Do what you think right with them.

Your niece

Mary.

SEVENTEEN

Rose folded the letter and looked up at Susan with great sadness in her eyes

"Oh, what a sad story. Your poor, poor, niece."

Susan nodded and took the letter.

"What are you going to do with it now?" Rose asked.

"I suppose I should show it to DCI Whitaker. If nothing else, it might point him to the killer but I'm still a bit confused about the other note left on my walkway. Based on the content of this letter what has that got to do with Mary's death?"

"I haven't a clue other than the fact that it's a biblical reference which makes me think that it is connected to the Mennonites. The reference to an eye for an eye and a tooth for a tooth could suggest that Mary's death was in retaliation for someone else's death, and that someone would have to have some connection to you. Boy, it's all a bit complicated, isn't it?"

Susan was just about to answer when the tasting room door burst open, and Renee appeared. She walked over to the women and said, "Oh, I thought that Tom would be here today?"

Rose looked at Renee.

"No, my name was on the schedule for today. Toms at the Marina working on his boat. Did you want to see him for any specific reason?"

Rene said smugly, "Well, he did such a good job of putting up my bookshelves in my apartment I just wanted to thank him again."

Susan looked at Rose and she could see her friend bristling. She needed to intervene quickly. Grabbing the small block of cheese she'd been dicing she said,

"Is this the last of the cheese, Renee or is there some more somewhere?"

Renee looked at Susan and frowned, "I think there's another block in the fridge if you look there?"

Rose had composed herself and began pulling out wooden flights ready for the wine tastings.

" Is there anything else, Renee, as we really need to press on. There's a tour bus due at twelve and we need to prep for forty people."

Renee got the hint and left the room. As soon as she'd gone Rose exclaimed loudly,

"Tom never told me he was putting up shelves for that that… that woman. I really do not like her, but Tom seems blind, he's always defending her."

"Yes, well, it's obvious that you don't like her and really, I don't blame you. She nettles me too and I don't know why. There's something about her that I just don't trust. Watch out Rose that she doesn't get her claws into Tom, beware."

Rose nodded. Yes, she would have to keep her eyes open and watch Tom like a hawk.

Their conversation was interrupted by the sound of a bus pulling up outside. The winery tour was about to begin.

EIGHTEEN

Jeff arrived at the OPP incident room a good half an hour before the scheduled team meeting. He needed time to think and to study all his notes if he was to see what it was that he was missing. Looking at the rather empty whiteboard he homed in on the artists impression of the man that Andrew from the Black Dog had spoken to.

The drawing showed a man, possibly in his late thirties, square jawed and rugged looking which Jeff thought could also apply to any one of the local farmers in Huron County.

But this man, if he was their man, was a professional shooter. Very few people use Tikka T3 rifles unless they were hunters and even then, you had to have a sharp eye.

No, Jeff thought their predator was a professional marksman or trained paramilitary. As to the tenuous connection to the drug cartel, well the ring was busted six years ago, and the perpetrators were either dead or in jail now.

Where was the connection to Mary Malloy? Of course, there was Samuel and his son Joshua, neither of whom could be found yet. Far more likely that he would somehow be involved with the drugs than Mary.

Jeff scratched his head and let out a deep sigh. He could feel a migraine coming on. They always crept up on him when he was stressed out.

The sound of voices pulled Jeff out of his reverie, he stiffened his back and stood up tall and welcomed his team as they entered the room. When they were all seated, he started the meeting.

"Good morning, everyone, another day in paradise. So, let's be having your reports. Constable Elliot, let's hear what you learned about Isabelle Cabella and the drug cartel?"

"Constable Elliot stood up pulling his notebook out of his pocket and quickly scanning what he had written.

"Well, when Isabelle was first here in Goderich she went by the name of Deb Nock. She was in a polygamous relationship with Seth Miller and Sonia Miller. All three were sex therapists. Isabelle was convicted of murdering Juliet Carmichael and Seth Miller, and she was also behind the whole drug trafficking operation. Being the great granddaughter of the National Assembly President of Venezuela, who was also the kingpin of the Venezuelan drug ring known as the 'Cartel of the Sun', Isabelle was put in charge of the Ontarian drug market."

The team all looked suitably shocked. Constable Patel interrupted Constable Elliot impatiently, "So what happened to her?"

Constable Elliot coughed and continued, "Retired DCI Susan Parker apprehended Isabelle, and she was incarcerated and then extradited to Venezuela. I contacted Interpol to see if they could give us an update on her status and they got back to me last night. According to the Venezuelan authorities they reported that she had died in prison just two weeks ago. That's about all I've got, sir."

"Thank you, Constable, now Constable Patel, what did you find out about our victim Mary Malloy?"

Maya stood up and cleared her throat. She had her laptop open and ready for her to read the notes she had made.

"Mary Malloy was born to Joan and Mike Parker on their small holding on Bronson line down the road from the Mennonite School. She attended the Mennonite school until she was fourteen then transferred to the South Huron District High School in Exeter. Samuel Malloy also attended the Mennonite school and the two of them grew up together.

When Mary was eighteen, she ran away with Samuel where they set up home on a leased cottage opposite the Anderson's pig farm just outside of Listowel. They had one son, Joshua. Neither Samuel or Joshua have been found for questioning, in fact the whole Mennonite community around Listowel have closed rank and refused to say anything about the Malloy's.

I gathered most of my information from an old couple living on Bronson line. They knew Joan and Mike Parker quite well. According to the wife Mary's parents split up not long after she left home. Apparently, Mike died some six years ago, and Joan now lives in Toronto with her new partner. That's about all I managed to find out, sir."

DCI Whittaker looked thoughtful. Scratching his head he said, "Everything seems to be pointing back to the drug raid way back in 2018. I still don't see the connection to Mary Malloy's death and the note sent to Susan Parker. Any thoughts?"

There was complete silence in the room and then Constable Elliott tentatively put up his hand as if he was in a schoolroom.

"Sir, regardless of why the murder took place, should we not be concentrating on the perpetrator. Do we know anything more about him?"

Sergeant Jennings interrupted, "I sent the identikit pictures for circulation to the RCMP and Interpol yesterday and I'm still waiting to hear back from them, but if this is connected to the Mennonites, my guess would be that the murderer is one of them."

"But why? What is the motivation here?" DCI Whitaker said with another big sigh.

"I'm going to go and interview Susan Parker and get a firsthand account of the murders committed by Isabelle. I feel that there must be a connection here, particularly considering her recent death. In the meantime, keep searching team. We do need to find Samuel and the boy, Joshua. There are far too many loose threads here, we need to tie them all up. OK, same time tomorrow everyone."

The team disbanded from the incident room and went back to their desks. DCI Whitaker picked up his phone and dialled Susans cell number.

NINETEEN

Rose finished her shift at the tasting room and returned home exhausted. I'm getting too old for working, she thought to herself as she kicked off her shoes and padded into the kitchen. Lifting the kettle, she walked over to the sink and turned the tap on. A cup of tea would be just what she needed. Just as Rose was about to turn on the kettle, Tom appeared with old Ben in tow.

"Oh, hi, love. Have you just got back?"

"Yes, and I'm exhausted. I see you took Ben for a walk. Tom, why didn't you tell me that you helped Renee put up her bookshelves?"

Tom looked surprised, "Well, there's nothing to tell here, I did just that, I helped put up the shelves. What's wrong with that?"

He was beginning to sound defensive. Rose made the tea and then poured them both out a cup and put some digestive biscuits onto a plate. Carrying them over to the kitchen island she sat down to rest her tired feet and continued the conversation.

"There's nothing wrong with helping Renee, but I suspect she has her eyes on you, Tom."

Tom looked incredulous. "You must be joking. Renee, fancying me. No way."

"Look, my darling, believe me, a woman knows these things and I know that Renee has designs on you."

"Well, she might have designs on me, but I certainly don't have any feelings for her. Honestly, Rose, I think that you're imagining it all."

"Mark my words, Tom, she's set her eyes on you. So just beware. Don't worry, she knows that I'm on to her, but seriously Tom, don't be so naive."

Tom snorted, picked up his cup of tea and a digestive and left the kitchen. Rose could see that he felt miffed, but he had to be warned. Susan and she had discussed the situation, and they were both in agreement that Renee was up to something. Forewarned was like being forearmed and Rose most certainly would not let Renee steal her husband away from her.

Tom came back into the kitchen soon afterwards and asked if there was anything she wanted done in preparation for Abby's stay. Jessica was driving down from Montreal with Abby while Ella stayed with Rob.

"Oh, yes, could you make up the bed in your study. Abby can stay there for the two weeks and Jessica can sleep in the sun lounge for the weekend. Tom, should we book tickets for Huron playhouse, they've got Cinderella the pantomime starting next week. Do you think Abby might be a bit old for that now?"

Tom thought for a minute, "Maybe we should just ask her before we book anything, love."

"Yes, you're right. OK, now I'm going to make Abby's favorite chocolate cake and some oatmeal cookies. What have you got on?"

"Well, I've taken Ben for his walk, I fixed the boat and now I'm going to put my feet up in the sun lounge and read my book."

TWENTY

Susan had just stepped foot in her condo and was about to pick Fluffy up when her phone rang. Putting the cat down she answered, "Susan Parker speaking." It was DCI Whitaker wanting to meet up with her to discuss the Mennonite murders. Susan didn't want to go out again and so she suggested that DCI Whitaker came round to her condo. She would make them both a cup of coffee and she could at least put rest up her poor aching feet. Standing in the tasting room hour after hour really was not good for her. They arranged to meet in thirty minutes time.

Susan went into the kitchen followed by Fluffy who rubbed up against her and purred loudly. "Yes, I know you want some food." Susan said as she reached down to retrieve the empty bowl from the floor. She filled it up with a mixture of dry and wet cat food and put it on the cat-mat ready for Fluffy to devour. With that done, she opened her cupboards to see if there were any cookies. All she could find was a packet of spaghetti and a couple of cans of soup. Now if this was Roses kitchen, Susan thought wryly, I'd be putting out scones and homemade cookies. She let out a deep sigh thinking to herself that a visit to the supermarket beckoned.

Susan did, however, have some good Guatemalan coffee freshly ground from the Shop Bike coffee shop in the village. She filled up the kettle and put 4 scoops of the fragrant coffee into the French press. With that done she went upstairs to her bedroom and freshened up adding a light touch of lipstick and a whiff of perfume. She was back in the kitchen just as the kettle was about to boil. DCI Whittaker's motorbike could be heard growling up Jowett's Hill a few minutes before he arrived at Susans condo.

Standing on the doorstep with his ginger hair all messed up from the biker's helmet, he waited for Susan to open the door. Although he had popped over a few days ago to pick up the note, it was the first time that he'd really looked at the Harbour Court development. Nestled beneath tall pine trees the condos blended in almost organically.

With wood sidings and tastefully designed windows the net result was a very attractive settlement. He wouldn't mind living here himself, he thought as Susan opened the front door.

"Wow, that was quick. Come in DCI Whitaker."

Jeff stepped in and looked around the light foyer. "Please call me Jeff."

Susan smiled, "Yes, only if you call me Susan." and with that settled he followed her into the cozy sitting room.

"This is lovely, so light and airy." Jeff said, "Gengus would love it."

Susan looked interested; she knew nothing about Jeff's private life. "Who is Gengus, is he your partner maybe?"

Jeff laughed, "Well, he is my best friend, but I'm afraid there ends our relationship. Genghis is my pet iguana."

Susan looked flabbergasted, "An iguana. What a strange pet for anyone to have. What made you get an iguana? "

Jeff smiled as he said, "Well, after my divorce, I wanted some companionship, but one that would not be demanding or need too much looking after. I just happened to see Gengus in a pet shop and the rest is history."

"But lizards are not exactly warm and cuddly companions." Susan laughed and went to pour out the coffee. Over her shoulders she said, "Oh Jeff, I've got something for you. A letter from my niece Mary. You're going to find it very interesting."

The next half an hour was spent with Susan giving Jeff an update on the whole case history of the Mennonite drug bust. She concluded with, "Isabelle was one smart cookie, but a dangerous person to deal with. She murdered three people and almost killed my friend Rose Blair. It transpired that she was the kingpin of the whole Ontario drug cartel, although Lydia Klassen dealt with the practical application by collecting the drugs from each farm."

Susan paused before continuing,

"It was a very tough case to crack. But let me talk about the contents of this letter."

She handed Jeff the envelope.

"Mary's friend Jane came around yesterday and gave it to me. She had apparently been instructed by Mary to deliver it to me in the event of her demise. You'll understand more when you read it. Look I'll go and make a fresh pot of coffee while you read it."

Susan got up and padded into the kitchen. She noticed that Fluffy had jumped onto Jeff's lap and was purring away contentedly. Jeff read the letter and at the end he exclaimed,

"Wow, what a story. I never knew that the Mennonites treated their women like that. It's horrific."

Susan had come back into the living room holding a fresh pot of coffee which she put on the tray.

"Yes, it is awful, although I believe not all Mennonites are the same. Most live in peaceful harmony and just don't want any outside interference. I'd hate to tar all Mennonites with the same brush."

Jeff scratched his chin as he thought.

"So, that explains how she escaped, but we haven't been able to find either her husband or her son. They seem to have both vanished off the face of the earth."

"In my policing days, we would always say, follow the money." Susan said. "If Samuel was in charge of selling the emeralds and distributing the proceeds to all the drug mules, it would make sense to follow that trail."

"But we need to find Samuel first." Jeff said.

"Have you put out a missing persons post yet?" Susan asked.

"No, but that should be a priority now for Samuel and his son Joshua. Tell me, Susan, did you ever meet the man yourself?"

"I did, briefly, at my grandmother's funeral. In fact, I think that was the very last time that I ever saw my niece other than on the day that she died at the golf course."

"Where was the funeral?"

"Oh, it was in Exeter, my grandparents lived in Exeter. My uncle, Mary's father, lived on Bronson line very close to the little Mennonite school which is not far from the Huron Ridge nurseries. In fact, Mary went to that school until she was fourteen and then she went to High school in Exeter. I think that Samuel went to the same Mennonite school. That's how they met. I know my aunt worked at the mink farm in Varna and sometimes in the school holidays Mary worked there too."

Jeff interrupted her, "Did you say a mink farm? That's interesting, is it still in operation?"

"No, I think that it closed about four years ago. I really don't know much about it; all I know is that there were several mink farms in Huron County. One in Clinton, another in Seaforth. It was a big business certainly in the 1930's and still going strong into the 1970's. By the time my aunt worked in Varna, the minks were being sent mostly to Denmark, Russia and China, very few were made into fur coats here in Ontario."

"So let me get this straight, your niece Mary grew up on Bronson line where she went to school with Samuel. She worked with her mother occasionally at the mink farm in Varna and then she ran away with Samuel and joined the Mennonite community near Listowel."

Susan nodded her head. "Yes, that's the gist of it. She gave birth to Joshua a year later and that's all I know."

Jeff stood up startling Fluffy who appeared to have fallen asleep on his lap.

"I'm sorry, I didn't mean to upset your cat, but I really must be off now. Thanks so much, you honestly have filled in many of the blank spaces, and this letter is pure gold."

Susan smiled, "I never did ask you how all your inquiries are going? I heard from Andrew in the Black Dog, that you got an artist over to try and capture the likeness of the strange man he served on the day of Mary's murder. You don't have a copy of the picture, do you?"

Jeff thought for a minute, "Actually, if you follow me out to my bike, I can give you one, it's folded up with the rest of my notes in the back carrier under the pillion seat."

Susan followed Jeff out to his bike. She ran her hands over the metal form sighing deeply.

"This brings back bittersweet memories. My ex, Tony, was a biker and totally mad about his Harley."

Jeff looked embarrassed; he liked Susan but wasn't sure how to take her. Reaching inside his pillion seat he pulled out a folder, inside a was a piece of paper nestled amongst other notes. He handed it over to Susan.

"Here you are. Let me know if he reminds you of anyone."

Susan looked down at the pencil sketch. It showed a good-looking man with a square jaw and a thatch of dark hair. He looked like Ernest Hemingway, well, at least a young Ernest.

"Thank you, I'm sure Rose will be interested to see this drawing. Right, see you sometime soon." Susan said as she returned to her condo.

Jeff stood there awhile contemplating the retired DCI Parker. What a woman, he thought, a cracker of a woman at that.

TWENTY-ONE

The following morning Tom got a panic call from Renee. "Oh Tom, one of the wine vats is leaking and there is wine all over the floor. I can't see where it's coming from." She sounded very stressed.

"Hold tight, Renee, I'll be right over."

Tom turned to Rose who was busy making a large saucepan of cauliflower soup.

"I'm going to have to go and help Renee, love, there's wine leaking out everywhere. Look I'll be as quick as I can."

Before Rose could say anything, Tom had gone leaving her wondering what was going on.

Tom found Renee in the processing room, she was holding a mop and a bucket. He could see straight away a steady trickle of red wine dripping from the seal where the spigot was attached to the tank. The floor of the processing room had been designed to collect wash water from the tanks sloping to a central drain in the middle of the floor so why exactly had Renee grabbed a mop and a bucket? Tom walked over to the offending tank. It looked as if one of the seals had gone. Looking at Renee he could see that she was distraught.

"Aw, don't look so worried, Renee, I'll soon get this fixed. What were you going to do with the mop and bucket?"

 Renee rushed over to Tom and put her arms around him and began to kiss his cheeks.

"Whoa...." Tom said uncomfortably, "There's no need for that. I'll have it fixed in a jiffy if you can find me a wrench."

He looked over to the corner of the room where most of the tools were kept. Renee looked up at Tom with tears in her eyes, "Oh, Tom, I don't know where I'd be without you."

Tom felt so awkward that he fairly pushed past her and in a couple of short strides had reached the tools and picked out the wrench that he needed. He preceded to tighten up the tap, it would hold for awhile, hopefully until he could get a replacement seal. The trouble was it would be impossible to replace it while the tank was still full of wine.

They would have to pump the wine out of the tank to do the repair work. Tom audibly sighed, it was going to be a big job, and he honestly didn't have the inclination or energy to do it. Maybe it was time that Renee and he had a serious talk about either selling the winery or getting a full-time manager in to run the place.

Rose and he were ready to retire and smell the roses again or at least spend more time in Antigua. Thinking about Antigua, Tom smiled to himself. They had spent three glorious months in their house on Dickinson Bay, and it had been three months of totally vegging out on the beach or around the swimming pool, lazing in the sunshine and doing very little else. Maybe next year they would extend their stay to four or perhaps even five months. He would ask Rose what she thought.

"OK, Renee, this will stop the leak for now. Fortunately, this tank full of Marquette is almost ready to be bottled. Let's set a date aside next week to bottle, we've got Abby coming down today from Montreal, but she can come and help too."

Renee looked at Tom with her big brown eyes and once again gave him a big hug, "Thank you, Tom you are my guardian Angel and my hero too".

"Well, I must get back to Rose." Tom stuttered as he turned to head out towards the car park. "I'll be in touch about setting a date for bottling and in the meantime, I'll order in a new seal for the spigot."

He drove off quietly relieved to be leaving Renee. She had come on to him and it made him feel thoroughly awkward, plus the fact that he realized that Rose had been right all along.

TWENTY-TWO

DCI Whitaker rode his bike into Clinton from London that day and was full of high spirits. Reading the letter from Mary had supplied much needed information which had filled many of the gaps in the investigation. He was keen to share this with his team.

Stopping off at Tim Horton's he purchased five coffees and a box of assorted doughnuts. It would be his treat today.

Jeff was the first to arrive which he liked as it gave him time to decompress and order his mind for the meeting. Looking at the white board with its meager offerings, Jeff went to pull out his folder to study the artists rendition of the possible hitman. It was then that he remembered that he'd given his copy to Susan Parker. One of the team would have to print off another copy to stick on to the whiteboard.

They had found a picture of Mary with Samuel and Joshuah in her house and that was now attached to the board. He picked up a green marker pen and started to draw a picture of emeralds which looked more like a collection of green blobs.

Constable Patel entered the room and walked over to the whiteboard.

"What have we here, Guv?"

Jeff laughed, "Aha, all will be revealed when the rest of the team gets here. Oh, there's a coffee over there for you and some donuts. My treat."

Soon the whole team was assembled, and Jeff took his place at the head of the table,

"Good morning, everyone, I've got some breaking news for you all in the form of a letter written by the recently deceased Mary Malloy."

There was a gasp in the room and Maya said in a low voice, "That's so creepy, sir, a letter from the dead, it's like a horror movie."

Jeff smiled, "Mary wrote this before she died knowing that her days were numbered if the elders in the Mennonite community discovered her secrets. Let me get copies made and then I suggest you all read it so you can form your own conclusions as to Mary's state of mind."

After distributing copies to everyone he re-read the letter himself and at then waited until everyone was ready to discuss the contents.

"Right, any questions?"

Maya shot up her hand, she was itching to get in the first words, "Two things, Guv, firstly, your collection of green blobs on the whiteboard, I presume that's supposed to represent the emeralds?"

Jeff winced, he knew that he was no artist, but his picture wasn't that bad, surely? He muttered, "Yes, they're meant to be emeralds."

Maya smiled, "OK, now my second question is, how did Samuel sell them and to whom?"

"That is for you to find out, all we know is that he sold them to a jeweler in London.

 Sergeant Jennings looked up, "Sir, should we be putting out a missing persons warrant for Samuel and Joshua? It strikes me that Samuel has a lot to answer for."

"Yes, you're right, Sergeant and a good idea too. Can you get onto that, also post it on Interpol. Now where are we with tracking down the identity of the man seen at the Black Dog on the day of the shooting. I'm of course referring to the artists impression that we put together. I know you've sent a copy to the RCMP and Interpol, but have we circulated it around the community? I gave my copy to Susan Parker so can you print off another one after the meeting and stick it up here on the whiteboard.

Also team, we still haven't got any closer to finding our victims killer. There can't be many people out there who own or who have access to Tikka T3 rifles, they're quite rare.

Constable Brown and Elliott, can you start with a search of the National Gun Registry and print off a list of registered owners. I know it's a big ask but we need to start somewhere. And also, while you are at it put out the word with the local rifle clubs."

Jeff looked at the whiteboard again and then pointed to the picture of Mary Malloy, " Susan Parker managed to fill in a little more detail about her niece Mary, she apparently worked with her mother at a mink farm just outside of Varna on Parr Line, I don't think the farm had anything to do with the drug cartel but it did close down shortly after the cartel was broken up and about the same time that young Mary left Samuel. Sergeant Jennings, can you track the owners down and see if there's any possible connection and ask about Mary and her mother.

Right, that's all for now. I feel that we're getting a little warmer, keep digging team and bring back some good results for me."

The team disbanded leaving Jeff still looking at the white board. They were still missing something, and it was niggling away at him, just what was it that they were missing?

TWENTY-THREE

Rose looked at herself in the full-length mirror in her bedroom. She hadn't seen Jessica or, for that matter, Abby, for almost a year now and she knew that her daughter would be scrutinizing her. The trouble was spending three months in the Caribbean had caused her to gain quite a lot of weight with all the meals eaten out at the many local restaurants and of course being very lazy and not doing much at all other than swim and sunbathe. On the bright side, she still was quite tanned and looked healthy enough. Rose changed into her favorite bright yellow sun dress, brushed her shoulder length hair and applied a little lipstick.

Looking at her watch, she called up to Tom, "They'll be here any minute now, Tom, are you going to change?"

He had returned from the winery that morning in a foul mood and had barely said a word at lunch and had skulked off with Ben for a walk. Rose wondered what had happened at the winery but was too preoccupied with Jessica's imminent arrival to start a conversation with Tom.

At five o'clock Jessica pulled into the driveway and Abby jumped out and ran to her grandma. Rose held her tight and then pulled back to have a closer look at her granddaughter. She was much thinner than last summer and had grown at least two inches taller. Before her stood a young woman, not the young gangly girl that she had known.

"My, oh my, you have grown up so fast, my darling, and you look fabulous." Rose kissed Abby and Tom came over and gave her a hug while Jessica pulled out a small suitcase from the back of the car. Tom went to help her and all four of them walked into the house.

"Now Abby, we've made-up the bed in the study for you, and Jessica, you can sleep on the sofa in the sunroom for tonight. I've made your favorite chocolate cake, Abby, would you like some now?"

Abby shook her head, "Is it gluten-free, grandma?" Rose glanced at Jessica, then Abby. "When did you quit gluten, Abby?"

"All my friends are gluten- free and I'm also thinking of becoming a vegetarian."

Rose and Tom rolled their eyes, and Rose couldn't help but say, "But I've made your favorite oatmeal cookies and the chocolate walnut cake that you love, can't you just go gluten- free once you get back to Montreal?"

"She has her own mind, mom." Jessica said as she grabbed a couple of the cookies and put the kettle on.

"So, mom, I heard on the news, that a young woman was killed on the golf course at the White Squirrel. Isn't that where you joined the Women's Golfing League?"

Rose looked uncomfortable. She just knew what was coming next. Jessica was so predictable.

"Tell me mom, please tell me that you were not involved?" Jessica's voice had taken on a shrill edge to it. Rose remained silent, instead of answering her daughter she grabbed Abby's hand and said,

"Let's go down to the beach and get some fresh air, we'll leave your mother to chat to grandpa, OK?"

Ten minutes later, Rose and Abby were sitting on the beach sorting out stones. Every year when the girls came to Bayfield, they would paint rocks and display them in Rose and Tom's back garden. It had become something of a tradition.

"Of course, when Ella comes, we can collect some more, but these will be my special rocks." Abby said solemnly.

"So darling, was it really bad at school? You know that girls of your age can be very mean, but you will have to learn to grow a thick skin because there will always be mean people out there. "

Abby looked serious, "But grandma, the pictures they posted of me were not even me, someone put my face on another persons bikini clad body," and then she paused and Rose thought that she was holding back tears, but she continued, " The next load of pictures were of me posing naked, but I swear it wasn't me, the same thing had been done as before, my face had been superimposed onto a nude model. Nobody believed me when I told them."

"What a dreadful thing. Oh Abby, I'm really, really, sorry. Did your parents contact the police as this is a very serious matter."

"You know mom wanted to, but dad said that it would only make matters worse."

"Well, I'm going to speak to my friend Susan Parker, she used to be a Detective Inspector in the Serious Crimes unit. She will be able to maybe give you some advice. Hey, but in the meantime, you need to forget about all of that and enjoy your stay with us. I've got a few plans to run by you. Firstly, I bumped into Ryan from the Bluestone Wakeboard Park, and he said that he'll give you a personal lesson if you want and he's free tomorrow. We could both go, and I could sit and watch your performances."

Abby smiled, Ella and she had visited Windmill Lake Wakeboard Park, but that was several years ago and now that had closed, and a new park had opened on Telephone Line. Ryan was now the manager at the park and Abby loved him.

"Oh grandma, that sounds so cool."

Rose smiled, that sounded more like the old Abby, she thought as they both stood up ready to walk back to Bayfield Terrace. "Oh, and Susan said if you fancy a hot tub this afternoon, you're welcome."

"Yeah, I love hot tubs. Ella and I've been bugging mom and dad to get one."

They reached Rose and Tom's house and immediately Rose knew that she was in for a lambasting from her daughter Jessica.

"Mum, dad just told me that you and Susan Parker were there at the scene of the crime when that poor woman was murdered. How do you do it? You're like a magnet for murder."

"Well darling, I don't intentionally go looking for it and that woman as you so put it, was actually Susan's niece, Mary."

Jessica looked abashed, "I'm sorry, I didn't know. That's terrible."

"Talking of Susan, she's invited us around to use her hot tub. I thought that we'd pop over after supper. I don't think that you're invited Tom, it would just be us girls."

"I'll stay with dad, mom, I didn't bring my bathing costume and I'm not a fan of hot tubs."

"OK, then it will just be us, Abby, and of course, Susan."

After a lovely dinner, Jessica and Tom shooed Rose and Abby away saying that they would clean up.

Soon they were knocking on Susan's door and were met by Ian who had his sports gear on.

"Are you going somewhere, Ian?" Rose asked.

"Yes, I'm on my way to play Pickleball. Enjoy your time in the hot tub, Susan's in the kitchen opening a bottle of wine."

Abby and Rose walked in and found Susan who was in the process of pouring out two glasses of wine. "And what would you like, Miss Abigail?"

Abby smiled, "Just water, please. Can I go and change in your washroom?"

"Go ahead, we will be out on the patio."

Rose followed Susan outside and sat on one of the patio chairs. There wasn't much space as the hop-tub took up most of the area.

"Oh, by the way, Susan, did you meet with DCI Whitaker?"

"Yes, he came here, and I gave him Mary's letter and told him a bit about her early years living on Bronson line and how she had met Samuel."

"Have they made any progress on the case?" Rose asked.

"Well, they've put together an artist's impression of the man Andrew spoke to at the Back Dog. Look, I'll show it to you."

Susan disappeared back into the house just as Abby stepped out onto the patio. "Wow, this is the biggest hot tub I've ever seen."

Susan returned holding a piece of paper, on it was a sketch of a man.

"Handsome, isn't he?" Susan said with a chuckle, "It's his strong masculine square jaw line."

Rose looked at it and Abby peered over her shoulder.

"He looks like a farmer." she said.

Rose folded up the paper and put it on the chair as Susan lifted up the hot tub cover. "Want to give me a hand, Abby?" Susan said.

Between them they soon had the lid off the hot tub and Abby hopped in.

"Are you coming in, grandma?" asked Abby. Rose nodded and pulled off her sun dress to reveal a one-piece floral-patterned swimsuit.

Susan proceeded to strip off her clothes and entered the hot tub stark naked. Abby stared open mouthed, and Rose added "I should have warned you, Abby, Susan always goes buff in the hot tub."

They all laughed, and the tension was broken.

TWENTY-FOUR

After Rose and Abby had gone, Susan, who now had just a bathrobe covering her otherwise naked body, poured herself out another glass of wine and settled down on the sofa with Fluffy cuddled up beside her. She pulled out her phone and punched in Ian's number. She knew that he would probably be nursing a beer at the Albion or Black Dog as his pickle ball game would have finished almost an hour ago.

"Hello, love," he answered before Susan had said anything, "Have they gone?"

Susan smiled, she knew that Ian was reluctant to be home while Abby and Rose were in the hot tub with his naked fiancé. He was basically a very shy man.

"Yes, they've gone, it's just Fluffy and me here now and I'm sitting here virtually naked and waiting for you."

Just as Susan said this the doorbell rang, "Oh, hang on Ian, someone's at the front door. I won't be a minute." Susan slipped her phone into the pocket of her bath robe and went to the front door. It was probably just Amazon dropping off a delivery, although it was rather late for that now at 8:00pm.

She opened the door to find two stocky looking men standing there. One sported a scraggly, ginger beard and was dressed like a farmer in rather grubby overalls, the other man looked younger and was wearing denims and a 'T' shirt, but his feet were clad in very dirty boots and there was a distinct odour of pig manure emanating from both.

"How can I help you?" Susan asked politely, wondering who the heck the farmers were.

The younger man stepped forward and Susan suddenly began to feel quite threatened. She went to push the front door closed but found that the younger man had thrust his booted foot into the door jam.

"Not so fast, lady," he said with a strong guttural accent," we need to know where the emeralds are."

"What emeralds?" Susan said feeling genuinely nervous, "What on earth are you talking about?"

"Oh, don't play the innocent with us," the older man growled, "you know too well what we're talking about. Your niece Mary still had them in her possession, and we believe she would have left them to you. Now hand them over, they are ours."

At the mention of Mary, Susan's eyes widened. *'Were these her killers'*, she thought.

"My fiancé will be home any minute now, so I suggest you leave. I don't know what you're talking about so leave me alone."

Susan hoped that Ian was listening into this conversation, she'd left her phone on, and she prayed that he hadn't ended the call.

Before she had time to think, the older man grabbed her by her neck and the younger man produced a dirty cloth soaked in chloroform which he pushed against Susans face. Within minutes she went limp.

The old man lifted her up like a sack of potatoes and carried her over his shoulders to a grubby white pickup truck parked across Susan's driveway. She was unceremoniously dumped on the back seat of the truck and the two men jumped into the front and drove off leaving a scattering of manure on the asphalt behind them.

Ian, who'd been privy to the whole event through Susan's cell phone, was totally shell shocked. *'What on earth just happened'* he thought. He tried calling back on Susan's cell several times but kept going straight to voicemail.

He pulled himself together, disconnected his last call to Susan and tapped out DCI Whitaker's cell phone number.

Jeff was just tucking into a big bowl full of chicken chow-mien. On the table in front of him were various dishes he'd ordered to eat in at the 'Lucky Palace' Chinese restaurant in Clinton. Their food was always good and the service very quick. He knew that he should have been on the road back to London by now, but his stomach growled and somehow the thought of waiting at least another hour before he ate dinner was not in the least bit appealing. Unfortunately for his waistline the Lucky Palace had become his regular eating place, so much so that Grace, the owner, now greeted him by his first name.

The chow-mien was delicious, he was just about to dig into the succulent sweet and sour chicken, when his phone rang. Swallowing quickly Jeff answered,

"DCI Whitaker speaking."

A panicked voice fairly shouted down the phone,

"They've taken her. You must come quickly before it's too late."

"Slow down, slow down. Let's start with your name." Jeff said trying to calm the agitated man whose voice sounded vaguely familiar.

"My name is Ian Green and they've taken my fiancé, Susan Parker. Please, you must come quickly."

Oh yes, Jeff thought, that was Ian Green's voice, but what was he saying about Susan Parker?

"Who has taken your fiancé?"

Ian painstakingly relayed his conversation with Susan and then the subsequent dialogue he had overheard between her and the two men.

"So, you see they've taken her. I've tried calling her phone but all I get is her voicemail. I reckon her phone has either been turned off or she has no service. You must do something."

Ian's voice had a desperate edge to it that pulled at Jeff's heartstrings.

"Listen, Ian, I'm going to head over to you now. The good news is that we should still be able to track Susan for a limited time through her phone unless they find her phone and remove her SIM card. I'll be with you in 10 minutes."

Jeff put his phone down and called out to Grace,

"Could you pack this to go please as I must leave now; oh, and put it on my account, thank you."

Within five minutes Jeff had passed on information on Susan's phone to the office with a request to locate her service provider and her device and was kitted up and on his bike driving like the wind over to Susans condo in Bayfield. He felt like a knight in shining armor off to rescue the damsel in distress, just who am I kidding here, he thought and smiled wryly.

Susan moaned and opened her eyes slowly, just where was she? It was the smell that gave her location away, that and the sniffling and grunting of what surely had to be pigs. She was tied with rope to a metal post in the corner of a barn and her mouth was covered by duct tape. Her bath robe barely covered her body. Suddenly, the barn door opened, and her two abductors appeared. They marched over to her and stood aggressively hands on hips looking down upon her. The bearded man spoke first,

"So, where are the emeralds?"

Susan knew that she had to play for time and the only way to do that was to try to talk the men into some sort of rational sense.

With a quick flash of his hand the younger man pulled the duct tape from Susan's mouth and gave her a hard slap on her face.

"Lady, you'd better start talking, Hank here don't have no time for swanky ladies like you."

He was leering at Susan's body which was partially exposed by the gaping bathrobe that barely covered her body.

"So, I'll say it one more time and then you'll regret not answering me truthfully, where are the emeralds?"

Susan decided that she would come clean. "They are in a safe deposit box at a bank. That's honestly all I know."

The older man groaned "Those f****** emeralds belong to us, so now little lady, you're going to have to go to the f****** bank and get them and hand them over to us. Do you understand?"

Susan nodded, "But the bank is closed right now." she said meekly.

"Well, you'll have to stay here until the morning. Which bank are we talking about?"

"The RBC branch in Exeter." Susan answered, "I have the deposit box key, but not here with me. It's in my Condo and without it and the authorisation Mary sent me that's the only way to get into the box."

The bearded man growled, "You better not be ****** with us, so listen this is what we're going to do. Tomorrow morning we're going to go back to your condo, pick up the key, and then we're going to drive to Exeter. Am I making myself clear?"

Susan nodded her head, she just prayed that Ian would come through. She must remain calm, she thought.

"I do need to pee," she said plaintively," and I'm hungry and thirsty."

"Quit making demands, bitch." the younger man growled, "if you promise not to scream or shout, we'll leave the duct tape off your mouth, but the minute that you yell out, the tape will go straight back on."

The older man smiled, "but we'll untie you briefly and you can go pee behind that stall," he pointed to with a grimy finger at a wooden trough in the other corner of the barn, "and don't try any monkey business."

They cut the duct tape off her ankles and wrists, and she tried to stand, but immediately fell again. Her legs had gone numb, and it took some movement to get her circulation going again.

Susan hobbled over to the stall and, crouching behind the box, she surreptitiously pulled her cell phone out of her pocket.

Mercifully the two men hadn't thought to look for a phone on her and it still had some power, and she knew that if the police were onto it they would be able to use triangulation to locate her. Should she try to call Ian?

Susan decided not to take that risk, instead she hid her phone underneath a bale of hay and then continued to do a pee.

Hobbling back to the men she put out her arms to be tied again forcing herself to submit with no argument. It was better to let them think that she was passively accepting her fate. Soon she was tied back up to the metal post and the two men left her, presumably to go back to the farmhouse for the night.

Susan resigned herself to her situation. She was confident that she would be found within the hour.

TWENTY-FIVE

Jeff arrived at Harbor Court just fifteen minutes after leaving Clinton. He had already called in Susan's telephone number and just needed Ian to confirm her service provider. It was probably Bell, he thought as he knocked on the front door. Ian appeared and opened the door and immediately Jeff could see the poor man was in torment.

"Ian, can you confirm which service provider Susan uses? Is it Bell or maybe Rogers?"

Ian paused and then answered, "I'm pretty sure that she's with Bell, why do you ask?"

"Well, it will speed things up for triangulation purposes. The server provider will provide the current or last known location of her phone and hopefully we'll be able to find exactly where they've taken her."

Ian's face immediately registered relief.

Jeff had already texted through Susans cell number and followed up by confirming her service provider. He put his phone away and patted Ian on his shoulders.

"We'll find her mate, don't you worry."

A few minutes later his phone gave a ping, and he opened a text with a link that in turn led to a map of Huron Perth county showing a blue dot.

"Here look. As I thought Susan's phone is almost exactly where I thought it would be. Looks as if it's on the way to Listowel. I'm off now, it will take me almost 30 minutes to get there. Stay calm, Ian, and hopefully she'll be home very soon."

With that, Jeff put his helmet back on, jumped on his Harley and throttled up the engine. He had disappeared by the time Ian had closed the front door.

It took Jeff less than thirty minutes to get to the last known location of Susan's phone. He killed the engine of his bike and walked, pushing the Harley the two hundred or so metres to his destination. A large barn loomed ahead with an old farmhouse to one side.

There were lights on inside the building, although the barn was cloaked in darkness.

Jeff stopped and surveyed his options. He strongly suspected that Susan was in the barn and probably tied up. It was still twilight; the sun had only just set in the past few minutes. Jeff decided to wait until it was completely dark, it would be far better to be in darkness when entering the premises. He would aim to go in about twenty minutes. Leaning his Harley up against a tree in the corner of some bush, he sat down to wait and wondered if he should call for backup or not?

Susan had managed to angle her head so that it was resting against the metal pole. Her hands and feet were tied, and a thick rope secured her body to the pole. Any thoughts of escape by undoing the ropes seemed impossible. Susan wondered if the men would bring her any food or water to drink. As if answering her prayer, the bearded man appeared at the entrance to the barn carrying a bowl of something and a bottle of water.

Jeff, alerted by the sound of a door being opened, watched from behind the hedge. A sturdy bearded man appeared from the farmhouse carrying what looked like a bowl and a bottle of water. He saw him cross over from the farmhouse and enter the barn and waited for him to come out again.

Susan smiled at her abductor as he put the bowl of what looked like chili on the floor beside her.

"Thank you, but how can I eat this with my hands tide up?"

The man obviously hadn't thought about this and so he pulled out his knife and sliced through the duct tape around her wrists. "Here you are. Now eat up and drink your water because this is all you're getting and make it snappy."

 Susan was indeed starving, she spooned down the chili, which was remarkably tasty, in no time at all.

"That was delicious, did you make it yourself?"

The bearded man smiled, "Yes, I like to cook." He sounded quite pleased with himself. "I always put chocolate and cinnamon in my chili".

Susan was surprised. She, herself not being a cook, was constantly impressed by the creativity of people who liked to cook. "Wow, chocolate and cinnamon in chili. I've never heard of that before, but it works, it's simply delicious."

She handed the empty bowl back to the man and drank half the bottle of water down in one thirsty gulp. Afterwards, she wiped her mouth with the back of her hand and stretched out her wrists to have them tied up again. Kill him with kindness, she thought, behavior modification 101.

After tying up Susan's wrists and collecting the bowl, the bearded man headed out of the barn and closed the door behind him which immediately cloaked the cavernous space into darkness. Susan resigned herself to an uncomfortable night still harboring the hope that she might yet be rescued, sooner rather than later.

Jeff watched as the man, only a silhouette against the light of the farmhouse, entered the barn and another 10 minutes later he reappeared closing the barn door behind him. Jeff waited another 10 minutes before creeping up to the barn and slowly opening the door. Entering the building, he was immediately greeted by the pungent smell of pigs. It was as he'd guessed all along, a pig barn. Closing the door behind him, he switched on his flashlight. Sure, enough he could see Susan tied up to a metal pole with her wrists and ankles secured by duct tape. The look of delight mingled with surprise, spread over her face as she whispered, "Jeff, you better be quick, either one of them might return any minute now. Here, cut off the tape around my wrists and I'll help undo the rope around my waist. Hurry,"

Jeff fumbled in his pocket and pulled out a penknife, he hastily cut the duct tape off Susan's wrists and ankles and helped her untie the knot around her waist. Within five minutes she was free.

"Follow me," Jeff said.

"Oops, I almost forgot my phone." Susan said pointing to the far corner of the barn where some bales of hay sat behind a wooden stall.

Jeff turned to whisper, "Hurry," as Susan stumbled over to the bale of straw. Her legs felt wobbly and numb, but she managed to grab her phone and get back to Jeff who had turned off his light and had opened the barn door.

"Right, my bike is parked behind that tree at the side of the road, we're going to have to push it down the road a bit before I can give it some throttle. OK, are you ready, let's go."

The two of them ran down the drive keeping in the shadows of the bushes each side. They reached the Harley and Jeff started to push the bike with Susan at his side. Fortunately, it was a cloudy night and there was no traffic on the road. After about five hundred metres Jeff jumped onto his bike and beckoned to Susan to climb on behind him. She managed to straddle the leather pillion seat, her bathrobe flapping open revealing her nakedness underneath. *'No time for modesty'* she thought as she leaned forward and grabbed Jeff around his waist as he opened the throttle and headed for home and to her beloved Ian.

TWENTY-SIX

Rose and Tom woke up to a beautiful morning. They could hear clattering in the kitchen and the next thing Abby was standing in their doorway holding two mugs of tea. "Mom's gone for a run, so I thought I'd make you both some tea."

"Oh, thank you, darling, come and sit on the bed and join us." The three of them sat in companionable silence and then Rose said,

"Right, I spoke to Ryan at the wake board park, and he said to come over for ten and then he can give you his undivided attention, a private lesson no less."

Abby beamed, "I remember Ryan. He's so handsome."

Rose looked at Tom and they both smiled. This was their old Abbey back from the brink, they both thought, as they finished drinking their tea. Ben came ambling into the bedroom, he could no longer jump up onto the bed as his arthritic legs and hips wouldn't allow it, but Abby crouched down on the floor and gave him a big hug. "I love you, old Benny boy," she whispered. Ben had been a big part of Abby and Ella's childhood, but now at 15 he was an old dog and would probably not make another year.

"OK I'm going to get up and get us all a big breakfast and then you and I, young lady, are going to the wakeboard park. Tom what are you going to do this morning?"

"Jessica wanted to go for a sail before she heads back this afternoon."

"Well, we have a plan, so let's get going." Rose said as she disappeared off to the bathroom. Soon Jessica returned and joined them all in the kitchen where Rose was scrambling eggs and frying up bacon.

Abby, you're in charge of the toast, Tom you can make the coffee, and Jessica, you can lay the table." Rose commanded as the bacon sizzled in the pan.

Afterwards, the clutter of dishes signaled the clean up of breakfast and the beginning of the day's activities. Tom and Jessica prepared to go sailing while Abby got her swimming gear sorted out.

"Are you going to go in the lake, grandma?" Abbey asked.

"Oh honey no. While you are wakeboarding, I'm going to lie on a sun bed and read my book. I'll be watching you though."

They arrived at the Bluestone Wakeboard Park just before ten. It was situated in a disused quarry and because of the limestone, the water was as blue and sparkling as a bag of sapphires.

There were only four cars in the car park. Rose pulled in next to a black Audi. "Nice car." Abby said and then she was off to find Ryan. He was standing by the dock next to the cable machinery used for wakeboarding. A man was out balancing precariously on his board. Abby and Rose held their breath as he just about managed to stay upright.

"Oh, grandma, I know Ella and I came out last year, but we just stayed in the water park. I'm not sure I'll be able to do it, it looks awfully difficult."

Ryan came up to them and smiled, "It's Abby, isn't it?"

Abby blushed, "Yes, my grandma booked a lesson for me, but I'm a little bit frightened, it looks very scary."

Ryan laughed, "Ah, everyone says that, but believe me, by the end of your lesson you'll be standing up on that board, I promise. Now if you come with me, I'll get you kitted out with a wet suit, life jacket, and helmet."

Rose knew that Abby was in good hands, she could relax and leave Ryan to do what he did best; teach her granddaughter confidence.

She walked over to a large umbrella and sat down on a Muskoka chair beneath it and, pulling out her book, glanced up at the wakeboarder still managing to stay upright. He was a good-looking man in his 30s, quite rugged, he looked vaguely familiar to Rose, but she soon forgot about him when Abby appeared in the water strapped onto the wakeboard with Ryan by her side.

"Look, grandma, I got up, and Ryan says that I'll be riding next."

Rose gave a thumbs up sign and continued to watch the man on the board.

"Ryan, do you know who that man is," Rose asked, pointing to the lake.

Ryan squinted with his hand up to his eyes. "Oh, that's Eli, he's a regular, comes everyday for a couple of hours. Why, do you know him?"

"No, but he just looks familiar that's all," Rose said and forced herself to look away and concentrate on her book.

Half an hour later there were squeals of laughter to be heard as Abby attempted to stand up on the board and then promptly fell over. She climbed back on and tried it again; this time Ryan held the board firmly to stop it tipping. Abby got right back up, Ryan let go of the board and Rose cried out triumphantly.

"Well done darling."

Abbey fell in again and swam ashore to Rose. "That was such fun, grandma, Ryan says that's probably enough for the day, but next time he's going to hook the board up to the winch."

As Abby was talking, the man on the board paddled to shore and got out of the water. Abby and Rose watched him as he removed his life jacket.

"Grandma, isn't that the man in the picture that Susan showed us last night? Look, he's got that very square jaw.

Rose looked and now she could see what had been niggling at her subconscious. "Oh, my gosh," Rose thought, "this could be Mary's killer.

She reached for her cell phone and punched in Susan's number.

A very groggy sounding voice answered, "Susan Parker speaking."

"Susan," Rose whispered, "That man in the identity picture you showed us, well, I'm pretty sure he's here at the Bluestone Wakeboard Park. It looks as if he's about to leave. Should I follow him?"

"No, absolutely not. Rose, that man is a killer. Look, can you get his car license number, and I'll phone DCI Whitaker. Now Rose, don't whatever you do, let on that you recognize him."

Rose gulped. She had been rather staring at him a lot.

"Abby, just stay here while I go and get something from the car, darling."

Abby nodded and continued watching some other wakeboarders who were gliding across the water and then jumping over some rails set up in the middle of the lake. A kicker ramp was also in the water and one of the wakeboarders was about to jump off the ramp. Abby watched mesmerized.

Rose walked over to the car park and opened her car door. She knew that she had a notepad and paper somewhere. There had only been four cars in the car park when they had first arrived, one of them was Ryan's Venza, she could easily copy down the license numbers of the other three cars. She found her notepad and pen and walked slowly back to Abby, pausing every now and then to write another license number down discreetly. Halfway back to Abby, the man with the square jaw, passed Rose and smiled at her saying.

"Good day, ya."

Rose nodded at him and continued to walk on at an unhurried pace.

"Grandma," Abby said, "Are you okay, you look a bit shaken."

Rose took a deep breath and said quietly, "I must make another phone call, darling and then we should head back home.

A very sleepy sounding voice answered the phone, "Susan Parker, speaking."

"I've just sent you a text message with three license plate numbers. Can you send them on to DCI Whitaker and tell him that Eli is leaving now. Are you okay Susan, did I wake you?"

"Oh, it's a long, horrible, story, but I'll pass your message on to Jeff. You should go home too."

Rose was about to put her phone down when she remembered something Ryan had said, "Oh Susan, apparently Ryan says he's a regular to the park, comes two to three times a week."

Ryan had ambled up to them and, at the mention of his name, he looked at Rose quizzically. Rose smiled at him.

"That Eli fellow, do you know where he lives?"

Ryan answered, "As far as I know, he lives close to Listowel or somewhere like that, about forty minutes away."

"Thanks Ryan. Okay young lady, time for us to go." Turning to Ryan she said, "That was great, Ryan."

"She was a star pupil." he answered and patted Abby on her arm. She blushed and with her head down followed her grandma to the car.

TWENTY-SEVEN

Jeff was on his bike driving to Clinton feeling decidedly knackered from the previous night's exploits, when he received the phone call. He pulled over to the side of the road and took out his cell phone.

" DCI Whitaker speaking." There was silence on the other end of the line and Jeff was about to end the call when a timid female voice said,

"I know where Joshua is. He is with my sister in St Jacobs. Find Flora Krupps and you will find the boy."

The call ended abruptly, and Jeff looked at his phone to see who had called and how long the call had taken. The user ID was hidden, and the call had lasted less than one minute so it probably originated from an unregistered phone. It would be almost impossible to track down the caller's number but based on the content of the call he had a pretty good idea of the identity of the caller, and they now had a good chance of locating the son.

Arriving at the OPP station, Jeff was keen to share his news with the team but as usual he was the first one there and so he spent the time studying the whiteboard.

The picture of Samuel and Joshua drew his attention; they were both good looking men with quite distinctive, strong, square, jawlines. He compared the artist's rendition of the man Andrew had seen in the Black Dog and with the photograph of Samuel and Josh. There was a strong resemblance between the three, certainly in the shape of the jaw. Jeff felt his spine tingle. They were getting closer to solving this murder; he could really feel it.

Although he was thoroughly exhausted from the night before, Jeff felt a degree of satisfaction over how the events of the evening had unfolded. He had called the Listowel OPP as soon as he had Susan safely back in Bayfield and before making the long drive back to London and had told them about the abduction. He had also contacted the OPP forensic identification unit who were sending a team to the farm to collect evidence.

Jeff was waiting for feedback from the Listowel OPP office who had sent armed officers to the farm to secure the scene for forensics and arrest the two men. They were currently in custody in Listowel and awaiting questioning.

The team trickled in and soon was seated around the conference table. He welcomed everyone and then preceded to tell them about the phone call he had received from the mystery woman.

"So, you see, thanks to you, Sergeant Jennings, and your missing persons information, we finally have a lead."

Sergeant Jennings looked pleased with himself. "Yes, sir, well I just thought that you should know I printed out a dozen photocopies of the picture of Samuel and Josh and went around all the supermarkets in the Listowel area. I rationalized that most Mennonites don't have televisions or indeed any social media, they would be more likely to respond to a picture posted in a supermarket than anything else."

"Well, it worked, Sergeant, well done. Now I spotted something interesting," Jeff said pointing to the picture of the mystery man seen in the Black Dog and then pointing to the picture of Samuel and Josh, "Can you see the likeness?"

The team concentrated on looking closely at both pictures and then Maya said, "I can see that they've all got strong square chins, but other than that, I don't see it."

"Well, that's what I thought. It may be nothing, but it may be also something to keep in mind moving forward." Jeff said and continued, "we'll get back to that later, but let's continue with our reports. Constables Brown and Elliot, what did you find out about the Tikka T3 rifle?"

Constable Brown stood up and pulled out his notebook, "There are two shooting ranges around Listowel, one called The Listowel Rifle and Revolver Club, and the other is called The Shooting Academy. Unfortunately, I had no joy in tracking down any owners of a Tikka T3, they both said that it was not a rifle that any of their members used. They were reluctant to give me further information about their members once they knew I was police, citing privacy laws.

One of the men I spoke with did confirm that the Tikka T3 is a bolt-action rifle manufactured by Sako in Riihimäki, Finland since 2003. According to an article I researched on Wikipedia the T3 series received an overhaul in 2016 and the improved models were named Tikka T3x. The Canadian version of the T3 CTR is designated C19 and is manufactured by Colt Canada and used by the Canadian Rangers. Thus, the Tikka T3 would have been made in Finland before 2016 and would be pretty rare over here."

"Thank you, Constable, now Constable Patel, what did you find out about the emeralds?"

Maya stood up and tapped on her laptop before beginning to read,

"I checked out jewelers online and followed up on foot as not everyone had information on the internet. I swear I ended up walking half the streets of downtown London, and my poor feet were worn out. I did find one jeweler who specialized in semi precious gem-stones, particularly emeralds." Maya clicked on her lap top computer and turned it around to show the team a picture of a store front called 'Isaacs' which came up on the screen. The shop looked nothing special and had metal barred windows. Maya continued,

"Isaacs is located on King Street and the owner was most helpful. He told me that he had been buying emeralds from a supplier on and off for many years, but in the last four years the supply had been restricted to three or four emeralds a month. To begin with he would not supply me with the name of the vendor, but when I told him that we were investigating the murder of Mary Malloy, he changed his tune. In fact, he appeared genuinely upset to hear that she had been murdered. I asked what the monetary value the emeralds were, and he told me that they were Venezuelan emeralds of the highest quality and apparently ranked amongst the best in the world. The value of Mary's emeralds amounted to almost two thousand dollars a month. That's about it."

"Thank you, Maya, now anything else on the mink farms Sergeant Jennings?"

"No, sir, as far as I could find out the mink farm was closed four years ago. The owners have retired, and the minks are no longer. I couldn't find anything else I'm afraid."

"That's OK, Sergeant, now where to next?" Jeff sighed before continuing. He felt bone tired after the previous nights frenetic rescue of Susan Parker. He had finally crawled into bed at midnight having hastily fed Gengus some frozen mice and gulped down some of his cold Chinese take-away.

He continued talking to his team whilst trying to suppress a yawn.

"Now for my big news. Last night Susan Parker was abducted from her condo in Bayfield and driven to a barn near Listowel. I managed to locate her whereabouts and got her back home safely. Her abductors were Hank and Walter Wiebe, and they are now in police custody in Listowel and have been charged with her adduction.

I also received an anonymous tip off that Joshua is in St Jacobs staying with the sister of the person who called me. Her exact words were, 'Find Flora Krupps and you will find the boy'. Right now, however, we need to go over to St Jacobs and locate Joshua. He might be able to shed some light on the whereabouts of his father. Constable Maya, you can come with me, the rest of you keep digging. Sergeant Jennings, can you investigate the cold case files for unsolved deaths in the Listowel area, our man Samuel might just be one of those statistics. Right, Constable Patel you can drive, unless you want to ride pillion on my bike."

TWENTY-EIGHT

After Maya and Jeff left the OPP station in Clinton, they headed out towards Seaforth and Mitchell where they turned left towards Listowel. By the time they had reached the small town, Jeff had fallen asleep, Maya's constant jabbering had lulled him into a gentle slumber; it had been a full moon that previous night and Gengus had been restlessly prowling around his apartment. At one stage, Jeff had woken up to find his pet perched on the end of his bed just watching him. Maybe he was hungry, but it was quite a sight seeing him silhouetted against the moonlight just eerily watching him. Consequently, what with the previous day's escapades rescuing Susan and then being disturbed by Gengus and the full moon, Jeff had had little sleep and now was catching up in the passenger seat of Constable Patel's little car.

He was woken suddenly from his slumbers with his Constable shaking him.

"Sir, we're on the outskirts of St Jacobs, where are we to go now?"

Jeff had conducted a name search before they had set out and had found the Krupps farm listed on the Listowel to Guelph Road, two kilometres outside of St Jacobs.

"Keep going on this road and I'll tell you when we get there."

They could see a cluster of modest looking buildings coming up on the left. The giveaway was that there were no hydro poles leading to the properties. Many of the Mennonites in that area were traditional in as much as they went without any mod cons, including electricity. They were the horse and buggy brigade often seen on the highway in and around Waterloo.

"Here it is." DCI Whitaker said, pointing to a small white sided two- story house with an old peeling picket fence surrounding it. Pulling into the driveway, Jeff could see barns ahead and some old tractors. It surprised him that there would be any motorized vehicles.

They knocked on the front door and it was answered by a small woman dressed in a long grey skirt and black blouse; her dark hair was secured in a severe bun at the back of her head.

"Flora Krupps?" Jeff asked and he put out his hand, "I'm DCI Whitaker and this is Constable Patel. I believe your sister phoned in and told us that you had Joshua living here. Is that true?"

Flora looked taken aback and uncertain what to do or say, finally she nodded and said in a thick accented voice, "Come in officers."

They both entered the gloomy hall and were ushered into the living room which was equally stark and unwelcoming. She pointed to the sofa for her guests to sit and then she pulled up a hard backed chair.

"I am Joshua's aunt. Four years ago, we were asked if we could take Josh in as his father was on his own and unable to look after him."

"Where was his mother?" Constable Patel asked gently.

The woman looked unsure of herself, and Maya didn't want to frighten her anymore than she had. Flora paused before answering,

"His mother left my brother Samuel, and the elders of his community felt that it would be best if Joshua moved in with us."

DCI Whitaker suspected that she was telling a watered-down version of the truth. He asked her, "Have you seen your brother recently?"

Another pause and then Flora answered, "No, I haven't seen him for at least four years, we don't see many people officer, distances dictate our community. To visit family in Listowel would take almost half a day by horse and buggy and we don't have any phones to communicate with. It is our way, sir."

"Can we speak to Joshua?" Constable Maya said, "Does he know that his mother's dead?"

There was a hushed silence and Flora looked as if she'd seen a ghost. It was obvious that she herself had not heard of Mary's death.

"When did she die?" she finally whispered.

"Four days ago. She was murdered on the golf course at St Josephs."

It all seemed so incongruous to think that Mary Malloy had once been part of this closed community of Mennonites. Looking at Flora in her plainclothes, her hair severely pulled back in a tight bun, it was hard to imagine the attractive Mary embracing such hardships.

DCI Whittaker pulled himself up from his reveries and continued his conversation with Flora. "You obviously have no phone in the house so how did you contact me?"

Flora blushed and answered quickly,

"Actually, it was my sister who did that, and it was easy. She used the public phone in the supermarket. While her husband was busy at the meat counter, she told him that she needed to use the washroom and then went and used the public phone to call you."

"But why did she contact me, she must have known that we would find you?"

"Officer, I'm a law-abiding citizen and my sister saw no reason why you shouldn't know that Joshua was alive and well and living with us."

"And you really don't know anything about Samuel? You see, everyone in his community is saying nothing, they've closed ranks. All we wanted was to notify him of his wife's death, but instead we've hit a brick wall. Thanks to you, we at least know that Joshua is safe. Can we speak to him?"

"Joshua is at school, in fact, he'll be home any minute now. Officer, if I may, can I please tell him myself about his mother?"

"Of course. Did you know Mary well?"

Once again, a deep silence filled the room. "I only met her twice, once at their wedding and she seemed so young and happy, then the second and last time I saw her, was at my grandma's funeral. Joshua, Samuel and Mary were all there. That was about five or six years ago, and she didn't look so happy then, but there again we were all at a funeral. "

Just then the front door burst open, and a young man appeared. He was the spitting image of his father Samuel. He rushed into the living room at first not noticing Maya or Jeff.

"Oh mom, I've been chosen for the basketball team." He spoke with the same guttural accent, a form of low Dutch. Flora gave him a hug and turned him to see her guests, "Josh, these people came to see you. They wanted to ask you about your dad."

Joshua looked bewildered, "But I haven't seen him for years, why ask now?"

Good question, Jeff thought as he signaled with his eyes to Maya that he would go first with the questions. "Your aunt will fill you in Joshua, but for now, we just want to ask you if your father had any problems with the elders of your community, particularly after your mother left?"

Joshua looked defiant and he shouted out, "She is no longer my mother, do you hear me, she left my father and me and that was the end of her. Do you understand?" Tears had welled up in his eyes as he threatened to cry. Flora put her arms around him and pulled him to her chest.

"I think that you should go before Abraham gets back."

Constable Patel pulled out the identity kit portrait of the man seen at the Black Dog and showed it to Flora, "Before we go, do you know this man?"

Flora's body stiffened as she shook her head and then Joshua looked up and over towards the portrait. "Hey, that looks like Uncle Eli."

DCI Whittaker turned to Flora, "Well, does he look like Eli or not? I must remind you that withholding vital evidence is a crime, madam."

Flora nodded, "Well, I'm not sure. Eli has the same square jaw, but I'm not totally convinced. Why? What has this man done?"

Ignoring her question Jeff continued, "Could you give me his address, please."

Flora was silent and Eli looked quizzically at her while Jeff and Maya waited for her answer.

"He lives somewhere in Listowel and that's all I know so please can you leave Josh and I in peace."

Jeff nodded and indicated to Maya that they should go. Before closing the front door, he pulled out his card, handing it to Flora he said, "If you think of anything else, here is my contact information."

They had just reached Maya's car when his phone rang.

"DCI Whittaker speaking."

It was Susan Parker sounding quite agitated. "Jeff, I just had Rose Blair on the phone, and it looks like she's found the man from the Black Dog, you know, the identikit man. She phoned me from the wakeboard park where he was just about to depart. Rose managed to get three different license plate numbers, she wasn't sure which car was his, but she found out that his name is Eli and that he is a regular at the wakeboard park. I forwarded the license plate numbers for you to check out and I'm sure a simple licence number search in the Ontario database will come up with his name and address."

"Heaven's, Rose has been busy, tell her thank you from me and thank you for getting hold of me so quickly. How are you feeling this morning?"

"Oh, I'm fine, just super tired. I know that I thanked you last night, but I just want to thank you again. You truly were my knight in shining armour."

Jeff chuckled as he put his phone away and relayed to Maya the gist of his conversation with Susan, but omitting the thank you part.

"I'm just going to contact the office and get his address and then I think Constable, we should head back over to Listowel."

Maya drove while Jeff contacted the office for a search of the vehicle license data base. They would get back to him in a few minutes.

Maya obviously had something on her mind, "Sir, how do we know that this Eli bloke isn't just a wake-board fan who also happens to maybe be Joshua's uncle. What is there to even connect him to the death of Mary Malloy?"

Jeff could see that she was clearly troubled, "Yes, you are correct. So far, we have nothing that would stand up in court, but let's see if we can connect a few more of the dots. Doesn't it seem coincidental that this Eli is related to a Mennonite and lives in Listowel where Mary and Samuel used to live."

"Yeah, but it's still too tenuous. We need some real facts. You'll be saying next that that you have a gut feeling."

She was of course right, Jeff thought. Maybe he was trying too hard to find a connection between the Mennonite community in

Listowel and to Mary's murder. They had had so little else to go on.

"Well, let's just wait and see, shall we." he answered lamely.

Five minutes later his phone pinged with a text message from the office. He read the message quickly and then conveyed the contents to Maya. "One of the cars identified at the wakeboard park is a black Audi belonging to one Elijah Klassen of 4 Victoria Street, Listowel. Now, the name Klassen, where have I heard that before?"

Maya answered quickly, "Sir, Lydia Klassen was convicted of running the drug ring in and around Listowel five years ago. She is currently serving a prison sentence at Kingston penitentiary."

"Oh yes, I remember now that Isabelle Cabella was the kingpin, but Lydia dealt directly with the Mennonites."

"OK, so we have Lydia and Eli somehow related, while you drive, I'll do a search on Lydia and her relatives and see what comes up."

By the time they reached Listowel and located 4 Victoria Street, Jeff had also discovered that Lydia was Eli's sister and that they had both grown up in the same Mennonite community.

Maya pulled into the driveway of a pleasant new and very modern townhouse situated in a large subdivision of similar houses, built on the outskirts of the town.

"This is certainly not a cheap house, is it, Constable." Jeff said, "He must be earning good money to afford this property."

There was no sign of a car in the driveway or any sign of life at the house.

"I'm calling a team meeting for 2:00pm, we need to get as much information as we can gather on Eli Klassen and fast. Head back to the OPP office, Maya, we have work to do."

They were speeding along Highway 23 when the phone rang again. Jeff answered brusquely.

"DCI Whittaker speaking."

It was Sergeant Andrews from the Listowel OPP.

"Chief, I think you need to see this. The forensic team have uncovered some almighty techy stuff at the farmhouse. Any chance that you can come out and take a look?"

"Well, Sergeant, as luck would have it, Constable Patel and I are only a few kilometres from the farm. We'll be there in five minutes."

Jeff turned to Maya and said, "Change of plans. Take the next left and head back towards Listowel. We're going to visit a farm."

TWENTY-NINE

After Susan had made her phone call to Jeff she decided to drive to Exeter. She still had the key to Mary's safe deposit box at the RBC bank, but also, she wanted to pop into Ellison Travel and pay the deposit on their upcoming trip to Paris. She and Ian were going to France for their honeymoon, and they'd booked everything through Ellison travel.

It was another beautiful June day and Susan was looking forward to her drive to Exeter. Rose and Abby were going to be bottling wine with Tom, and she might call in to Huron Estates winery on her return to see if she could help with anything. Renee was supposed to be helping until 2:00pm when Abby and Rose would take over in the tasting room.

Twenty minutes later Susan pulled up in the parking lot alongside the bank and entered the premises. After meeting with the branch manager to review the authorisation to access the safety deposit box and after signing some paperwork Susan was escorted to the secure vault where the boxes were located.

Finding the correct one, she opened it to find a small suede pouch. Inside were about twenty sparkling emeralds. Susan removed the bag from the box, put it in her purse and closed it. After signing out with the manager she left the building feeling as if she had just robbed a bank.

After that, she popped into Ellison travel and then ended up in Sobey's where, in the fresh produce section, she bumped into Jane, Mary's friend.

"Oh, hi Jane, fancy meeting you here." Susan laughed.

Jane smiled, "How's the police inquiry going? Have they got any nearer to finding the murderer?"

"Funnily enough, just today they got their first real break. Its still early days but based on several sightings of a stranger seen at several locations that correspond to the time of the murder, they believe they may have found the hitman."

Jane went quiet and her voice took on an edge. "Gosh, that was quick, who is he?"

"I don't know, but all I can tell you is that he goes by the name of Eli and lives in the Listowel area, oh and that he likes wakeboarding."

"That's sounds like an oddball account; how do they know that he is their man?" Jane looked intently at Susan.

"They don't know for sure that he is the killer. The police have been following a lead based on an artist's impression drawn from a description by someone at the Black Dog. Suffice to say the police are labeling him a 'person of interest'.

"Well, that's good news, then isn't it." Jane said sounding rather strained. She proceeded to fill her trolley with vegetables and fruit. She abruptly turned to Susan and said quickly, "Well I must be going, Susan, nice chatting to you."

Susan finished her shopping and went out to her car. She was feeling a bit preoccupied with what Ian had said to her the previous evening. He said that he would like them to buy a new house together for the beginning of their married life. That meant selling her condo. The family egg farm had already been sold and Olive, his mother was still very much enjoying herself living at Harbour Hill retirement home. Susan understood Ian's desire for a fresh start, but she did love her condo, and her hot tub. Could she move? She wasn't sure what to think. Being preoccupied, she missed the turn off for the winery and had to turn around at the Tim Horton's garage on highway 21 and drive back to Deer Ridge Lane.

She got out of her car and looked around, there were half a dozen cars in the car park, and she could see Rose's old Volvo parked behind the processing room. Walking towards the side door of the winery she could hear Abby and Rose laughing and Tom's deeper voice instructing them what to do.

"Oh, hi you lot, do you need any help?"

Rose looked up from labeling a bottle of wine and Abby laughed saying, "Grandma is hopeless, every label she's put on is crooked."

Rose laughed.

"Honestly, I must have wonky eyes because all the labels look straight to me."

Susan walked over and said, "Why don't I help Abby with the labeling while you help Tom with the bottling."

Soon they were all working in tandem, Tom bottled, Rose corked, and Susan and Abby put on the labels and attached the foil wrappers over the tops of the bottles. Soon they'd assembled and filled almost fifty cases from the vat.

"How many more to go, Tom?" Rose asked.

"Fortunately, this vat was only half full, otherwise we would be bottling well over twelve hundred bottles. We probably only have another couple of cases left to finish this vat. Do you want to take a break? Why don't you go and make us all a coffee while I finish up."

"Well, my legs are killing me." Rose said, "I wouldn't mind a little break. Shall we go into the tasting room and sit at one of the tables in there."

They left Tom bottling and traipsed into the tasting room where Renee was busy explaining to a group of people the intricacies of the different wines. You had to hand it to her, Rose thought, she was good at her job, very knowledgeable about wine and very personal with the public.

"I'll go into the kitchen and put the kettle on. What about you, Abby, would you like some milk or water."

"Just water, grandma." Abby said.

"Susan, you'll have a coffee with me, won't you or would you prefer a glass of wine?"

"No, I'll save having a glass of wine till this evening, but I will join you and Tom for a cup of coffee."

Rose got up and passing Rene she said, "Would you like a cup of coffee, Renee? I'm making a fresh pot for us."

Renee looked up and asked curtly, "Where's Tom? I could do with some help here."

She knew jolly well where Tom was, thought Rose, but she wasn't going to get into an argument.

"We're emptying the leaky tank and bottling all the wine. Another hour or so and we should be all done."

Susan, Rose and Abby returned to the processing room with a mug of coffee for Tom. He was just finishing off bottling the last of the wine and looked up triumphantly. "Last one done, all we have to do is finish labelling and packing the cases and then I can power wash the tank and get the spigot fixed."

"How many bottles did we get out of the container?" Rose asked.

Taking his mug of coffee, Tom took a big gulp before answering, "I just did a count, and I reckon we will fill fifty cases which is six hundred bottles of great tasting 2022 Marquette. How are things going in the tasting room?"

Rose pulled a face, "Well, Madame is moaning that she needs help specifically from you, Tom. I told her you were busy."

Tom winced, he was becoming increasingly aware of Renee's unwanted advances and wasn't quite sure how to deal with it all. As if reading his mind, Rose said, "I know that you're feeling uncomfortable with her Tom, it's time that we looked for an assistant to help her in the winery and leave you more time to enjoy the pleasures of life. You haven't played golf with Doug for a while now, have you? Talking of which, Doug really might hit it off with Renee, what do you think?"

Tom paused for thought. Doug had been widowed now for almost three years and after making a full recovery from a heart attack the previous year, he would probably welcome the companionship of another woman. Maybe he should invite Doug over to help in the tasting room and see what happens. He smiled and put his arms around Rose, pulling her in for a big hug,

"You know something, love, you might just be onto something," and he kissed her nose and patted her back. "Right now," he said, "let's get these last few bottles labeled and the foils put on and then home everyone.

Abby piped up, "Leave the labels, grandma, Susan and I will do those, you can do the foils."

Rose laughed and soon they were all busy finishing off the bottling and ready to go home to a slow cooked pork

THIRTY

DCI Whittaker and Constable Patel arrived at the farmhouse six minutes later. As they pulled up on the roadside outside the farm Jeff looked at the building closely. In the light of the day, it really looked run down and decrepit. The big barn loomed large and, as they stepped out of the car, the smell of pigs greeted them.

"Whoa, what a stink." Maya said as she held her nose, "Sir, is this where Susan Parker was being held?"

"Yes, but it was nighttime and almost pitch black. I didn't realize what a dump the place was until now."

They had reached the side door of the dilapidated farmhouse. Inside men in white disposable outfits mingled in the cramped and messy kitchen. One of them turned to speak to Jeff.

"Sergeant Andrews said you were on your way, but I didn't think that you'd get here quite so quickly. Slip on these shoe covers and gloves and follow me."

After donning the protective clothing they followed him through a small, dark and very shabby sitting room and into what looked like an outhouse.

Opening the door to the ramshackle building they were suddenly greeted with a blast of light. The room they had entered was nothing more than a state-of-the-art I.T. centre. Three computers were set up with multiple screens giving the impression of something straight out of NASA or some sci-fi movie.

"What the heck." Jeff said, "This is incredible."

Maya's eyes had lit up immediately she had seen the computers. She had always loved technology and considered it her calling. If it hadn't had been for her brother's untimely death, she would have gone to university and studied computer engineering, but instead she had vowed to try to seek out vengeance for her brother's murder by joining the Police Force. Now, she felt, her skills could finally be unleashed.

"Sir, can I have a closer look. Maybe see if I can crack the password and open up the system?"

"I tell you what, Constable, why don't I leave you here while I pop into town and interview those two scumbags. I should be back in about an hour. Will that be okay with you?"

Maya beamed, "Yes, Sir, this is great." And she sat down and immediately started tapping the keyboard, "See you later."

Jeff left Maya happily playing with the computers. He managed to hitch a ride into town with one of the SOC guys who was busy packing up his gear and loading it all into a white van.

Ten minutes later Jeff walked into the small OPP office in Listowel and asked to speak to Sergeant Andrews. A tall and very handsome officer appeared from one of the rear offices. He extended his hand to Jeff,

"Sergeant Andrews, we spoke on the phone."

Jeff smiled, "Yes, thanks for calling me so quickly. Now where are the two farmers? I want to interview them."

"Follow me. We have a small interview room at the back. I'll bring up Hank first. He will be your best bet for getting any information, the brother is almost monosyllabic."

Jeff was shown into a small white room which held a desk with one chair each side. Soon Hank appeared handcuffed to one of the officers who unlocked the cuffs and stood menacingly by the door while Jeff sat down and motioned to Hank to do the same.

Jeff took out his phone and pressed record.

"Hank Wiebe I am going to read you your rights. Listen carefully and answer me truthfully and you will soon be released. This interview is being recorded and will be considered part of your testimony."

Jeff proceeded to read him his rights. "Now, last night you visited Susan Parker in Bayfield. What was the purpose of your visit?"

Hank chewed his cheek and looked sullen. He was going to be a hard nut to crack, Jeff thought as he waited for the truculent man to reply.

Hank started to speak in a low guttural voice, "That bitch has something that belongs to me. I wanted it back. That's all."

"What exactly does she have?"

"It's none of your business."

Jeff had to hold himself back from shaking the man. He took a deep breath and calmly said, "

"Emeralds. I believe it was emeralds you wanted from Ms. Parker."

Hank's eyes shot upwards as he stared Jeff directly in the eye.

"Them emeralds are ours, not hers."

"I believe they were the property of Ms. Malloy, recently deceased niece of Ms. Parker, am I correct?"

Hank begrudgingly answered, "Yes, well, they still belong to me."

"So, you thought it was okay to abduct Ms. Parker, tie her up in your barn and interrogate her?"

Hank said nothing.

"Well, moving along. Do you know this man?" Jeff showed Hank a picture of Samuel Malloy.

Hank looked at it and grunted. "Yea, I knew him. Samuel Malloy, that bitches husband."

"When was the last time that you saw him?" Jeff asked.

Hank thought for a while and then answered slowly, "It must be at least four years ago."

"So back to the emeralds," Jeff said, deliberately changing the subject to try to throw the man.

"I told you they are our property, and she stole them."

"Who stole them, Ms. Malloy or Ms. Parker?"

Hank looked confused. "Umm, Ms. Malloy and then she gave them to Ms. Parker, so both those bitches took my emeralds."

"Tell me about the emeralds. Where did they come from and why do you have them in your procession?"

Jeff could see that Hank was beginning to waver, just a little more pushing now.

"Did they come from Venezuela or maybe Mexico, Hank, and were they by any chance in payment for a certain number of drugs passing through your hands?"

Hank looked shocked that Jeff should know so much about their operation. He looked flustered and suddenly unsure of himself.

"Um, I, we did receive emeralds in payment for work done, and yes, they were from Venezuela."

"And where did Samuel Malloy fit into all of this?"

Hank stuttered as he said, "He was part of it, that's all. Them emeralds were his as well as ours."

"Okay, we've established that the emeralds came into your and Samuel's hands, so how come Ms. Malloy got hold of them?"

"She stole them from her husband." Hank shouted, "The bitch stole them and gave them to her aunt."

"Okay, so now we're getting to the truth. So, tell me, Hank, why wait four years to retrieve the emeralds?"

Hank shuffled in his seat. Jeff could see that he was getting agitated. He waited in silence for the gruff man to answer.

"Well, we didn't rightly know where the bitch had gone. She just disappeared one day along with the emeralds."

"And what about her husband and son?"

"Well, they hung around for a bit, but then they disappeared too."

"So, when did you find out Ms. Malloy's whereabouts?"

"We heard that she had been murdered at some fancy golf course and that her aunt lived in Bayfield. It didn't take much searching to find that bitches address."

Jeff knew that he had probably got as much out of Hank as would have expected. It was time to get back to the farmhouse and find out about the computer equipment, but before he dismissed Hank, he turned to him and said,

"What are you doing with all that fancy computer equipment you have installed in your outhouse?"

Hank looked shocked and once again shuffled in his seat.

"That there, equipment is my brother Walter's business. It has nothing to do with the emeralds."

"Okay, that's all for now. We will be holding you both for a further 24 hours so relax and enjoy our hospitality." Jeff smiled as he left the shattered looking farmer to ruminate.

Back at the farm Maya had managed to navigate the system to the point that she finally found the right password access. "Bingo" she shouted out loud and made the one remaining officer in charge jump. Once she had access to all the files, she started to methodically go through them all.

One hour later DCI Whittaker arrived back at the farm having got a ride from one of the officers in Listowel to find Maya totally emersed in her work.

"Have you found anything of interest, Constable?"

Maya looked up and smiled broadly. "Yeah, I'm sure I'm onto something, but first, sir, can you smell something?"

Jeff sniffed the air, he could smell something rather whiffy, and it wasn't the ever-evading pig smell either.

"Yes, you're right, there definitely is a stink and it's coming from over there." He pointed to a side door. "I'll just go and investigate."

He entered a dark enclosed space adjoining the main farmhouse and adjacent to the shed containing all the computer equipment. The pungent smell was almost overwhelming as he stood there trying to adjust to the dark. Scuttling of feet and other rustling sounds seemed to surround him. Jeff grabbed his phone and turned on his flashlight. Cage upon cage containing little furry creatures were stacked against the sides of the building. Tiny, shiny eyes looked up at him and, in Jeff's imagination, pleaded to be released from the hell and torment of captivity.

I must phone up the SPCA, Jeff thought as he stumbled back to Maya and the relative freshness of the IT outhouse.

"Guv," Maya said as he coughed and wiped his mouth while taking big gulps of air. "Are you okay?"

"God, Maya, it's dreadful back there. There must be hundreds of little furry, rat like creatures caged up in the most unhygienic conditions. I need to call the SPCA."

Jeff dialled a contact number for the SPCA and after a brief conversation with the receptionist informed Maya that they would be sending an officer from Kitchener to review the situation as soon as possible.

"Well, sir, that explains something I've found on the computer. There are multiple orders for mink pelts from all over the world. Look."

She pulled up one order from Russia. The requisition was for two hundred pelts to be delivered by the end of the month.

"But that's not all, sir, there must be at least fifty different computer games logged into the server."

"Gambling games like poker?"

Maya pulled a face, "That's the strange thing, sir, all the games are the sort of one's that young boys tend to play. You know the type; all action, fast cars and shooting."

"And you said that the other files were pertaining to mink-pelt orders? How far do they go back?"

Maya tapped on the keyboard again and answered Jeff quickly, "It looks like the orders started about six months ago. The most recent one was received just a week ago.'

"Interesting. So, it appears that the two brothers are running an illegal mink farm. Wasn't our deceased Ms. Malloy employed at one stage at the mink farm in Varna?"

"Yes, if I remember correctly her mother worked there and Mary sometimes helped out."

"And Samuel and Mary lived just down the road. A co-incidence or what?"

Constable Patel glanced at her watch and said, "Guv, we better be going if we're to make the team meeting."

Jeff looked at the time and whistled, "Yes, let's go."

"Hang on a minute, sir, while I download these files onto my USB stick." Maya replied as she hastily plugged in the stick and patiently waited for the files to be downloaded.

THIRTY-ONE

Constable Patel and DCI Whittaker reached Clinton just in time to grab a quick coffee and bagel from Tim Horton's. The meeting was scheduled for two and they arrived at the OPP station at one-fifty by which time the rest of the team were already waiting for them.

Putting his coffee and bagel down Jeff started the meeting without preamble.

"Constable Patel and I found the missing boy Joshua, he's living with his aunt Flora and uncle Abraham Krupps, just outside of St Jacobs. It transpires that our person of interest in Mary's murder identified as Eli is actually Flora's brother and wait for it, he is also the brother of one Lydia Klassen. You may recall that the drug cartel that was broken up some six or so years ago in Listowel was run by Lydia Klassen and Isabel Cabella. Anyway, we drove to the address taken from his vehicle registration just outside Listowel in a new subdivision of townhouses, but there was no one at home. Now that we have his license plates and an address, we should easily be able to apprehend him. I've contacted Interpol to see if they have anything on him. Sergeant Jennings, have you anything to report?"

Sergeant Jennings pulled out his notebook and scanned his notes before clearing his throat.

"Yes, Sir, I searched my way all through the cold case archives for the Listowel area and bingo, I found that the body of a man believed to be in his early thirties was found in the Listowel reservoir a couple of years ago. His skull had been smashed in, and the body was in an advanced state of decomposition so at the time no identification was made. If this body is possibly Samuel and now that we know where his son lives it would be easy enough to get a DNA sample to confirm if the body is Samuel."

Jeff nodded his head, "Good thinking, Sergeant, can you get onto it. Now, any more information gathered?"

Constable Elliot spoke up, "I still can't see the motivation for the murder of Mary Malloy behind all this Sir? Is it drug related or what on earth is going on?"

Jeff replied slowly, "You're right, Constable, it's still unclear what's behind all of this, but what we do know is that Eli was seen shortly after the slaying of Mary Malloy and has been identified as being connected to one of the biggest drug cartels in the country. We also know that Samuel and Mary lived on a Mennonite community just outside Listowel close to where Eli now lives. We also know that Samuel was trading in emeralds and that his wife Mary was in an abusive relationship with Samuel and left him taking the emeralds she had purloined. Those are the facts that we know."

Just then a ping was heard and Jeff looked down at his phone. "I've just received some interesting news from Interpol. Eli Klassens was a member of the Springbok Mercenary Brigade; he is a trained sharpshooter and was working in South Africa for ten years. He returned to Canada six months ago.

Right, so that adds weight to our theory that Eli Klassen is our hitman, but why he murdered Mary Malloy is still a mystery. It feels as though we're making headway team. Okay, tomorrow is Mary Molloy's funeral. Sergeant, I'd like you to come with me and see if our man shows his face. Remember, he doesn't know that we are on to him and so we have that big advantage.

Now other news is that Constable Patel and I discovered something interesting at the farmhouse where Ms. Parker was held in the barn. The SOC people found an outhouse containing state of the arts computer equipment. Constable Patel was able to access the system, and she found some interesting files. It appears that the Wiebe brothers have been running an illegal mink farm. There were cages and cages of the little furry animals locked away in a dank and dark shed. I called the SPCA and am waiting to hear back from them."

Sergeant Jennings put up his hand.

"Yes, Sergeant." Jeff said.

"What have mink got to do with the emeralds and Mary's death, sir?"

Jeff paused before he spoke. "There must be a link, and my bet is that it involves drugs. Not sure how yet, but we're getting warmer. Right, we'll meet later tomorrow afternoon after the funeral."

With that the team dispersed, Jeff was left once again studying the whiteboard. "Why was Mary Malloy killed?" kept niggling at him.

THIRTY-TWO

The Trivet Memorial Anglican church was an imposing neo gothic building, built in 1888 and located on the Main Street in Exeter. Susan had driven past the building hundreds of times before but had never been inside. It certainly was impressive with a beautiful stained-glass window and the capacity to seat six hundred people. Today however, only the first three rows of the church were taken up.

A coffin sat on its bier with a single simple wreath of white roses nestled mournfully on the oak lid. Susan slipped into the fourth row of pews joining DCI Whittaker and Sergeant Jennings who had arrived earlier. She nodded to both and then looked around expecting to see Jane but couldn't see her anywhere. Maybe she was running late, Susan thought, but with only twenty people in attendance she would be hard to miss.

Susan observed an older couple sitting in the front row. They were presumably Mary's mother, Joan and her partner from Toronto.

The service began and was officiated by a vivacious looking minister heavily made-up with bleached blonde hair worn with jelled spikes, she looked like an elf and Susan was captivated by the incongruity of her appearance.

Her reverie was however, broken by the choir singing 'The Lords my shepherd," and everyone stood while a few quavery voices joined in. Mary's mother was beyond comforting. Tears rolled down her cheeks and every now and then her whole body heaved with great sobs. Susan wondered just how long ago it had been since she had seen her daughter and if they had ever reconciled.

Soon the hymn was over, and the eulogy began. It was obvious that the minister knew very little about Mary, but she did a valiant job and then four pallbearers appeared from seemingly nowhere and the coffin was led out, followed by the small congregation.

Susan squinted into the sunshine; she wanted to have a quick word with Mary's mother before she went off to the cemetery for the internment. Mary was to be buried next to her grandparents in the family plot.

A few people were busy giving their condolences to the mother. While she waited for her turn Jeff Whittaker came up to Susan.

"Short service," he muttered, "Are you waiting to talk to the mother? You know she wouldn't talk to us, in fact, she flatly refused."

Susan smiled, "I'm sure I'll get her talk to me, as I am after all a relative. Have you seen Jane anywhere?"

Jeff shook his head, "No, I was looking for her too. It's funny, I thought that she was Mary's best friend."

"I bumped into her in Sobey's yesterday and she seemed fine. She wanted to know if any progress had been made in the investigation."

"What did you tell her?" Jeff asked with just the beginnings of a tingling in his spine.

"I told her that you might have found the hitman based on a description of a man known to the police as Eli and that he lived in the Listowel area. That is actually all I know and that's only because Rose and Abby spotted him at the Blue Stone Wakeboard Park."

Jeff nodded and continued, "Oh and by the way we found Mary and Samuel's boy, Joshua, he goes by the name Joshuah Krupps. He's living with an aunt in St. Jacobs, just on the outskirts. Did you ever come across an Eli Klassen?"

Susan paused, "Well, we put away Lydia Klassen six years ago for the drug bust, but, no, I've never actually come across an Eli Klassen. You do realize that Klassen is a very common German name around the Listowel area."

Over Jeff's shoulder, Susan could see that Mary's mother was no longer engaged in conversation with anyone, this would be her cue to have a word. "Excuse me, Jeff, I'm going to chat to Mary's mother now."

Susan walked over to the distraught parent. Putting her arms out for a hug she said,

"Do you remember me? I'm Susan Parker, Mary's aunt?"

There was a moment when Susan thought that she saw a glimmer of recognition light up in her sad face, "I'm sorry, my memory is not what it used to be."

"Never mind, I just wanted to say that I saw Mary just shortly before she passed away and she seemed happy. I know that she left the family and joined the Mennonites, but I also believe she did that out of love for Samuel. You do know that you have a grandson, Joshua?   I've written down the address where you can find him should you want to become acquainted. He apparently is in the good loving care of his paternal aunt."

Mary's mother's eyes welled up again heavy with tears, she wiped her face with the back of her hand before answering. "Yes, I knew that she had given birth to a baby boy. He must be around fourteen now. It's strange to think that Mary and Samuel started dating when she was that age. You know they were inseparable. Samuel was gentle and sweet, not at all like his cousins, Eli and Lydia, who were our neighbors on Bronson Line. Eli liked to kill things, he would shoot squirrels and rabbits, and Lydia would curse and swear."

She paused before continuing, "And then there was Jane, the youngest sister. She was rather sweet and used to play with our Mary when they were young things, but when Mary and Samuel became an item, Jane withdrew herself from the scene and went off to live in London. Between you and me I think that Jane had a crush on Samuel and was as jealous as hell when Mary ran off with him." Joan's eyes opened wider as she appeared to remember something. "Of course there was that unfortunate incident at the mink farm."

"Oh, tell me about it." Susan said feeling a tremble of excitement bubbling up inside her.

"Oh, it was such a long time ago now, but if I remember rightly Jane and Mary were working Saturdays at the mink farm and Jane was fired for stealing money from the till. She claimed that it was not her, but Mary. Both girls were asked to leave, and we never heard anything more about it. Shortly after Mary and Samuel eloped together and Jane moved to London."

Susan squeezed Mary mother's hand and took her leave. She looked around for Jeff

Whittaker. Did he know that Jane was Lydia and Eli Klassen's sister? If Jane knew that the police had Eli down as a 'person of interest', then she would certainly have tipped off her brother and it's all my fault, Susan thought, remembering her conversation with Jane at the supermarket in Exeter.

It was no good, Jeff seemed to have disappeared, and Susan needed to be at the winery to help Rose and Tom. She picked up her phone and left a text message for Jeff and then she drove to Bayfield and to the sanctuary of Huron Estates.

DCI Whitaker had indeed left the funeral with Sergeant Jennings. They had a team meeting in Clinton to attend to and some news to relate to the team.

THIRTY-THREE

They were all seated and ready for the debriefing. Coffee and doughnuts sat squarely on the conference table and there was a general air of excitement. The chase was on and hopefully the case would soon reach an end.

"Good afternoon, everyone," Jeff said as he entered the room. "I hope that you've got some news for me, I certainly have some information to share with you all, but first, Sergeant Jennings, would you like to tell the team the results of your inquiry into the body found in Listowel dam?"

Sergeant Jennings pulled out a printed sheet of paper and started to read from it. It was a whole load of numbers which meant nothing to the team. Jeff interjected, "Sergeant, just summarize what is on that printed sheet please."

Sergeant Jennings looked embarrassed. He coughed and put the paper down and pulled out his notepad. "Well, I drove to St Jacobs and got a saliva swab from the young lad, Joshua. I put a rush on a DNA analysis and the results from his DNA show that he is a 99.9% match to the DNA taken from the body found in the dam. Thus, they are pretty certain that the body is indeed Samuel, Joshua's father."

"Thank you, Sergeant, so we have the cold case a step further to being solved. But now to the present. It appears that Jane, Mary's 'so-called' best friend, might also be a suspect now, along with her brother, Eli."

Jeff could see the look of shock on his team's faces. "Apparently Eli Klassen is also Jane Smith's brother as well as the brother of Lydia Klassen, our drug dealer. It appears that she found out that we were onto her brother, and it looks as if they have both done a runner together."

Constable Elliot put up his hand, "But, Sir, I still don't understand the motive? Why kill Mary and what about that biblical quote Susan Parker received? I just don't get any of it."

He did indeed look perplexed.

"Well, Constable, I received a text message from Susan Parker herself. She had been talking to Mary's mother at the funeral, and it transpires that although Jane and Mary were best of friends at primary school Jane became jealous of Mary when Mary and Samuel became an item. There also was an incident at the mink farm where Jane was accused of stealing some money and she tried to put the blame on Mary and both girls were fired. Shortly afterwards Samuel and Mary eloped, and Jane moved to London. It doesn't look as if they really were the best of friends."

"But why kill her?" Constable Patel asked.

Jeff continued, "Well, I daresay if Eli hadn't returned from South Africa our Mary would probably still be alive. Don't forget he's a mercenary and a pathological killer. If you consider the fact that their sister Lydia was put away for her involvement in the Mexican drug cartel and that the leading officer was indeed DCI Susan Parker, that might be the connection we're looking for. Any thoughts?"

The team all looked down at the table. If Jeff's hypothesis was correct, then they still had the killer in their sights.

Jeff continued, "So far, Jane has not been even remotely a suspect, but now that we know her relationship to Eli, it is obvious that she could be the instigator of all of this. It could have been Jane who told Eli exactly when they would be at the White Squirrel, likewise Jane could have supplied Eli with Susan's address. We cannot underestimate this woman. Now the big question is where would they hide? Any ideas?"

Constable Patel put up her hand, "Sir, they have loads of relatives in the Listowel area, that's probably where they would be laying low."

"Yes, you could be right, but they can't leave the country, and we've put out alerts for both of their cars, photographs have been issued and are circulating not only in Canada, but within Interpol. We will catch them of that I'm sure, but when is another matter."

Constable Elliot put up his hand. "Sir, what about Samuel's murder? Should we not be investigating that?

"I've been in touch with the Listowel police and they're sending in a team to investigate. Knowing how the Mennonites 'close ranks', I'm not holding my breath, but we can but try. OK, we've made much progress so go home and rest up, tomorrow we start operation manhunt."

Just as the team were dispersing Jeff received a phone call from the SPCA.

"Is that DCI Whittaker?" The pleasant-sounding voice asked.

"Yes, how can I help you?"

"My name is Julie and I'm phoning from the SPCA in Kitchener. You called in about the caged mustelids."

"Umm, mustelids? I'm not sure what you mean?" Jeff said perplexed by the strange word.

Julie laughed, "Mustelids are all part of the stoat, weasel, mink, polecat, and pine marten family, oh, and so are otters although they are a much bigger species. I'm calling to let you know that we found around five hundred mink and fifty stoats in the cages."

"Stoats?" Jeff said, "Why would anyone farm stoats?"

"Stoat pelts are more commonly known as ermine. In the past they were used as a soft lining for coats and hats, oh, and also royalty used to have ermine cloaks. Not so popular these days fortunately."

"Thank you, Julie. If you could send me a written report on your finding that would be great."

Jeff ended the phone call and thought to himself, why a mink farm?

THIRTY-FOUR

Susan found Rose, Tom and Abby in the tasting room of Huron Estates winery. They were busy cleaning up and getting ready to go home.

"How did the funeral go?" Rose asked her friend, and Susan told her all about Jane, Eli, and Lydia.

"So, you mean to say Jane arranged to have her friend killed? But why on earth would she do that?" Rose exclaimed incredulously.

"Well, according to Mary's mother, Jane was jealous of her relationship with Samuel."

"But that surely wouldn't warrant something as drastic as murder. There must be something more to it than that?" Rose bleated.

"Yes, well I've been thinking about that, and I think it's all tied up to that note I received. You know that Isabel Cabella died in a

Venezuelan prison just a week before Mary was killed. Well, Isabel was Jane, Eli and Lydia Klassen's niece, and Mary was my niece, so an eye for an eye, a tooth for a tooth, good Old Testament retribution."

Abby, who had been sitting quietly listening to Susan and Rose talking, looked positively shocked. Her eyes were as big as saucers and her face registered alarm. "Did you say that she murdered her niece?"

Tom came over to the three women with a tray of drinks just in the nick of time, wine for Susan and Rose, and coke for Abby. He put the tray down onto the coffee table and lifted his glass saying,

"I think that it's time to toast the bride- to- be. Are you getting excited yet, Susan. The big day is on Saturday."

Susan smiled. Trust Tom to change the subject. They shouldn't have been talking about Mary's murder in front of young Abby. The poor girl looked positively traumatized. Oh well, Susan thought, if nothing else it would take her mind off the horrid cyber-bullies back in Montreal.'

"How did your bridesmaid's dress fit, Abby?" Susan asked.

"Oh, it's perfect. I love it."

Rose smiled, "And my dress also is just right. Now, as maid- of- honour I must insist to being at your place on Saturday to help you get ready for your wedding."

Susan laughed out loud, "Honestly, Rose, I don't need any help."

"Oh, but it's traditional for the maid-of-honor to be there with the bride-to-be. Besides, I'm assuming Ian won't be there? Where is he going to stay when he gets ready for the big day?"

"He's going to his mom's place at Harbour Hill. He'll change into his suit and then drive Olive and himself over to the Little Inn, where he'll wait for the not so blushing bride."

"Right, well that's all settled then. Tom will bring Abby and himself over to the Little Inn and I'll stay with you and help you get ready and then we'll go over to the Inn together. The wedding is at five, so how about I come over to your place around three; is that okay?"

Susan pulled a face, but she knew when she was defeated. "Whatever you say, Rose, whatever you say."

A car pulled up outside the winery and Doug stepped out and opened the passenger door to Renee. Together, hand in hand, they walked to Renee's apartment. Tom watched from the tasting room window and smiled a huge smile. Renee had other fish to fry now, and Doug was welcome to her.

THIRTY-FIVE

Jeff finally had a bit of time to go shopping having managed to get home at a reasonable time. He loaded up his trolley with kale, cabbage and spinach for Gengus and salad stuff for himself. Picking up a ready-cooked chicken and a tub of potato salad he started to feel hungry. He hadn't eaten anything since the bagel and coffee he and his constable had shared before the team meeting and that was hours ago. Jeff called in at the pet store on his way home and picked up another packet of frozen mice and was promptly given a lecture from the owner of the shop.

"You know that lizards are herbivores, don't you?"

Jeff was taken aback by his tone of voice. Surely it was none of his business what he fed his pet.

"Umm, he does eat vegetables, but mice are his special treat," he replied lamely.

It was true, Iguanas were supposed to be herbivores, but Jeff had read somewhere that in the wild they might eat a mouse or two. Unfortunately, just like his sister and her spoilt cats, once she had given them a treat of canned cat food, they then promptly refused to eat their dry kibble. Gengus had made it known to Jeff that he loved mice and was basically indifferent to greens.

Jeff returned to his tiny apartment on Wellington Street in London. What it lacked in space it made up for in spades by its location. He was situated right opposite Victoria Park and within stones throw of the Serious Crimes Division HQ. As he entered his apartment, he could immediately see that the whole living room/kitchen area looked like a tsunami had passed through. Gengus was standing alert by the front door, but as Jeff entered, he scuttled over to his terrarium and climbed in looking innocently up to his master.

"Bloody hell, Gengus, what have you been up to?" Jeff shouted which was the wrong thing to do because Gengus hated raised voices He turned his back on Jeff and hissed.

"Oh, I'm sorry, mate," Jeff said, "I didn't mean to frighten you, but what have you been doing here?"

Jeff looked around again this time more carefully. Suddenly two things dawned upon him, firstly that he had not put down a piece of newspaper in the usual place in the kitchen as Gengus always went to the toilet in the same location. Secondly, in his rush to leave that morning he had not given Gengus any mice, instead he had thrown some wilted spinach and kale in a bowl which now lay tossed on the living room carpet.

It was obvious that Gengus was angry with Jeff and was letting him know in no uncertain terms that he was mightily cheesed off.

Jeff had just about restored some order to his living room when his phone rang. It was Constable Patel, and she sounded very excited.

"Sir, I think I've cracked it, I mean, the code. Our two brothers are definitely involved in drug trafficking, but here's the thing, Jane Smith is also involved. She deals with the shipping and packaging of the pelts which, if my guess is right, are layered with drugs"

"That's astounding. Great work, Constable. I think tomorrow morning we should pay a visit to Jane's house. I doubt very much if she's still around, I'm fairly convinced that she's on the run with her brother Eli. Look, why don't I meet up with you at her house in Exeter, say nine o'clock tomorrow?"

The following day Jeff deliberately gave Gengus more frozen mice than usual and dispensed with the greens. He had restored some order to his living room, and everything seemed back to normal again.

Leaving some classical music on for Gengus, "The Planets" by Gustav Holst was his favorite piece, Jeff closed his front door and hopped on his bike for the drive to Exeter.

Constable Patel was already parked on the side of the road in her little bright yellow car, "Bessie-the Beetle", if he remembered correctly. Jane Smith's house was situated in a quiet cul-de-sac in a well-maintained neighbourhood. Trees lined the street and hanging baskets containing brightly coloured geraniums and petunias were suspended by hooks on nearly every house on the block. Jane's home looked well loved and cared for. One thing that immediately drew Jeff's attention was the large, double garage which extended to the full length of the property.

"Have you knocked on the front door yet, Constable?" Jeff asked.

Maya stepped out of her car and ambled towards Jeff.

"No, I was waiting for you, sir."

"Right, well I strongly suspect that she won't be here but let's go and have a look."

Jeff was right, there was no answer to his repeated knocking on the door.

A man walking his dog stopped in front of Jane's house and called out to Jeff and Maya.

"She's not in. Left yesterday in a bit of a rush."

"Thanks," Jeff and Maya said in unison.

"Right, lets go and have a look at that garage." Jeff said and proceeded to walk over to the side door of the garage. He pulled out a set of skeleton keys and proceeded to insert one and wiggle it around. Trying the door handle and expecting it to open, Jeff was disappointed to find it was still locked.

"Do you think that we should wait to get a search warrant, sir?" Maya said.

"Umm, no, if it was her house rather than a garage then maybe I would be a bit more circumspect."

They both stood there a while pondering the situation and then Maya suddenly noticed a keypad installed, or rather hidden, behind the drainpipe.

"Sir, look there's a keypad here, looks new to me and, hey, there's a security camera aimed right at us up there."

Maya pointed to the guttering around the roof of the garage. Sure enough, there was a tiny camera mounted on a small bracket, and it was aimed at the entrance to the side-door.

"She obviously wants whatever's inside this garage to remain secure."

"If it's a recent installation," Maya said pointing to the keypad," then I'd like to bet that the installers used this year as a password."

Jeff looked bemused as he tapped in 2025. A loud click announced that the lock had been released, and they were able to open the door.

"You're quite brilliant, Constable." Jeff said as they entered the large space. Inside there were cardboard boxes stacked on top of each other and flat pack boxes waiting to be assembled.

"Shall we open one of these, sir?"

Jeff nodded and they both lifted one of the boxes off the stack onto the floor. It was not particularly heavy and, although it was taped up, Jeff was able to cut the tape with his penknife and open the box quite easily.

They both peered inside.

"It smells a bit musty." Maya said as she pulled out a pair of gloves from her pocket.

Inside on the top were stacked a dozen small mink pelts. Maya carefully lifted the top layer and pulling a face, she peered inside. Sure enough there was a second layer of little plastic packets of a white substance that looked remarkably like cocaine. They dug deeper into the box and found that every alternate layer was made up of packets of drugs.

"Let's open this box," Maya said pointing to a slightly different sized box from the first.

Inside the box were snowy white pelts, presumably stoat fur. Layered underneath the pelts were packets of white pills.

"My bet is it's fentanyl." Jeff said.

Maya and Jeff open several other boxes and by the time they had finished they had found cocaine, fentanyl, ketamine, and bromazepam.

"Wow, what a haul," Maya said as they carefully closed the last box. "But where are the Wiebe brothers getting these drugs from and what the heck is bromazepam?" Maya said.

Jeff answered her. "Bromazepam is used most commonly for anxiety and panic attacks as far as I recall."

"So, what now, sir?"

"I need to go back to Listowel after the team meeting and interview the other brother, Walter. According to Hank, the computer was all his baby. Not sure if that means this mink-farm was his sole business or not. I very much doubt it as the fella didn't seem to have too much on top, but you never know, still waters and all that."

Maya hadn't a clue what her boss was saying, but she nodded her head in agreement.

"I'll call this into the Exeter OPP right now before anyone else turns up as I'm sure someone somewhere is monitoring the camera. We should also have forensics come by and secure the scene and impound all these drugs and pelts; and while we are at it, we should also obtain a warrant to search the house. If anyone asks, then we gained entry to the garage as we had concerns for the safety and welfare of Jane Smith. Once they get here, we need to go. Good work Constable. I really feel that we are closing in."

THIRTY-SIX

DCI Whittaker and Constable Patel arrived at the team meeting just on time. Jeff had called an emergency meeting of his team even though it was a Saturday. He had no intention of making it a long meeting, but he felt that the team should be kept in the loop with the discovery of the haul of pelts and drugs stored in Jane Smith's garage.

All the officers were present and waiting to get started. He grabbed a marker pen and wrote the words PELTS and DRUGS in big letters on the white board.

"Good morning, everyone, I promise to make this as brief as possible, but Constable Patel and I uncovered some interesting material, and we think it might be connected to our case."

He proceeded to outline the drug bust and the connection to the mink farm.

"You see, the Wiebe brothers have been farming these poor little creatures and using them as a front to traffic drugs."

Sergeant Jennings coughed and tentatively put up his hand.

"But what have the drugs got to do with the murder of Mary Molloy and what about the emeralds?"

Jeff thought that he was beginning to sound like a stuck record and felt a degree of irritability towards his Sergeant.

"Well, the murder of Mary Molloy seems to be connected to Eli Klassen and his sister, Jane. Jane, it appears, has been acting as the packaging and distribution agent for the Wiebe brothers. We think that maybe Mary might have worked at the mink farm when it was first started up and before she left Samuel and ran away. She certainly had experience of working on a mink farm from her youth when she helped her mother working at the Varna mink farm. I aim to find out more after I've interviewed Walter Wiebe this afternoon in Listowel."

"I still don't get the connection between any of this, sir?" Constable Elliot said looking perplexed.

"I think, Constable that the emerald business has muddied the waters, so to speak"

Constable Patel rolled her eyes thinking to herself, Here goes the Guv again with his weird sayings.

Jeff continued, "The emeralds were in payment for the Venezuelan drugs over four years ago. Mary purloined the emeralds, secreting them away so that she would have something to live off when she left Samuel. We suspect that when the brotherhood, or whatever they were called back then, discovered that some emeralds were missing, they initially took it out on Samuel and that might have been the cause of his demise. We may never know. Hank and his brother Walter were determined to reclaim the emeralds which they thought were rightfully theirs. Hence Susan Parker's abduction. The drugs may or may not have any bearing on the murder of Mary Malloy. We won't know the whole story until we've apprehended Eli and Jane."

"Right now, I'm driving to Listowel to interview Walter Wiebe as according to his brother, Hank, the computer business was his baby. I need to know where the drugs have been coming from and the financial worth of the whole set-up. So, have a day off tomorrow and let's meet up again on Monday at nine a.m."

Jeff watched as his team members left the building. He looked at his watch. It was still only 10:30 am, with a bit of luck he would be able to get to Listowel by 11:00 am, interview Walter, and hopefully be back home by about 2:00pm. It was the last weekend of Wimbledon and Jeff was mad about tennis.

He jumped on his bike and drove to Mitchell where he took a left turn onto Highway 23 which took him directly to Listowel. Last time Constable Patel and he had gone via Wingham and Blue Vale, and it had taken forever to reach their destination. He clocked the time and realized that he had indeed reached Listowel in under thirty minutes.

Arriving at the OPP station he sought out Sergeant Andrews who promptly went to fetch the prisoner, Walter Wiebe.

Walter shuffled into the interrogation room and sat down with his hands retrained in handcuffs. He looked the worse for wear with his straggly beard all matted and his T-shirt stained with something, presumably food. His eyes looked bloodshot, and his face appeared all twitchy.

Jeff placed his phone on the table and began to read Walter his rights.

"Now, Walter, I've already interviewed your brother, Hank and he told me that the computer and the mink farm were all your business. Is this true?"

Walter looked a little confused.

"Please answer my question." Jeff persisted.

Finally, Walter coughed and said,

"Well, yes, I was given the computer in payment for me looking after them critters. I fed and watered them daily, but that's all I did."

"Someone must have killed and skinned them and dried the pelts. Was that you?"

"No, no, I would never kill them, I got to love them little furry mink."

"Well, who did the deed?"

Eli started to say something and then thought better of it. He stubbornly clamped his mouth shut.

"Who downloaded all those video games for you? Was it Jane?"

Walter's eyes widened as realization hit him.' "You know about Jane and her brother then?" he said incredulously. "They swore me to secrecy so how did you find out?"

"The dates of the transactions gave them away. We know that Eli Klassen returned from South Africa six months ago and we know that Jane is his sister. We also know that Jane worked at a mink farm when she was young and so she had some experience in that field. So, I assume Eli did the slaughtering, am I correct?"

Eli looked angry, "Yes, he culled one hundred of them just last week. There is an old barn at the far end of our property and that's where the pelts are hung up to dry. I refuse to go there. It makes me sick. Eli just laughs and feeds all the innards to our pigs. I can't bear the man. He is cruel and sadistic."

"Tell me about the packaging side of the business. How does Jane fit in?"

Walter looked down at the table and deliberated with himself. Finally, he looked up and said," I suppose you already know that her sister is Lydia Klassen, and she was incarcerated four years ago for trafficking drugs. Well, Jane managed to get a list of the drug suppliers in Canada, and she used that list to purchase the drugs. I swear I had nothing to do with any of that side of the business. All the pelts were sent to an Exeter address, presumably Jane's house and whatever happened to them after they left here, I have no idea."

"How were Eli and Jane paid for the drugs and pelts?"

"Once again I was not privy to any of that, but I suspect they were paid in Bitcoin or something like that, some sort of crypto currency, but hell, I don't know.'

"So, you want me to believe that your only payment for the operation was in computer games? I think that's stretching it a bit, don't you?"

"Well, it's the truth. Hank didn't want us getting involved and he made it perfectly clear that he would not be part of any dodgy business."

"How come Jane did all the business transactions from the computer set up in your outhouse? Why not use her own computer?"

"She didn't want her home computer compromised."

"So, what you're saying is she came to your farm and did all the business transactions." Jeff said incredulously. "How often did she visit?"

"Sometimes once a week, other times not so often."

"And she left the raising of the mustelids to you?"

"Umm, what are mustelids?" Walter said scratching his head in confusion.

Jeff smiled. He loved the word and had been determined to use it somewhere in the interview.

"Mustelids are all your critters; mink, weasels, stoats, polecats and even otter's."

"Oh, yes, well Jane didn't want anything to do with the farming aspect, neither did Hank."

"Let me get this clear. You farmed the animals, fed and watered them, let Jane and Eli use your farm as a base for a highly illegal operation, and you did all of this for nothing."

Walter shook his head, "I get to play computer games and Jane says that I can keep all the equipment. That's plenty payment enough for looking after the critters."

Jeff paused while he thought a bit. It was obvious that he would get no more from Walter and really, he already had a pretty clear picture of how the whole operation was being run. He stood up and beckoned to the officer standing by the door.

"I've finished here." he said, and with that Walter was dismissed and Jeff jumped on his bike and headed off towards London where his beloved Gengus would no doubt be patiently waiting and the sound of tennis balls thwacking across the courts was beckoning.

THIRTY-SEVEN

Saturday came around so quickly, Rose had barely any time to think about the fact that her best friend Susan, was getting married. She had known her for over forty years having been at Queens University together both studying English. Rose had met Tom and Susan had met 'the Jerk', his name had completely eluded Rose as Susan only ever referred to him as 'the Jerk'. She and Tom had got married as had Susan and the Jerk, but Susan's marriage had only lasted all of three years.

Since then, Susan had had a series of boyfriends, was engaged to Henri Le Bruin, a Sûreté du Québec officer, commonly known as the SQ, but he was tragically murdered after helping her with the Murder at the Croquet Club investigation. She had then married Tony, an undercover cop working for the 'drug-squad' in London and ironically helping to break open the Mennonite drug-trafficking case four years ago. That marriage had lasted all of two years. She sincerely hoped that her dear friend had now found the right man in Ian, the county pathologist.

That morning Abby got up and made Tom and Rose a cup of tea and bringing it into their bedroom, she had jumped on their bed crying out, "It's the wedding day, it's the wedding day, hip, hip, hurray, it's the wedding day."

Tom had opened one sleepy eye, glanced at the bedside clock, and had rolled over in bed and attempted to go back to sleep. It was only 6:00 am. Rose understood her grand daughter, it was just that she was so very excited and could barely contain herself. Rose recalled the conversation when Susan had asked Abby to be a bridesmaid and how excited she had been then.

"Oh, Susan, I've never been to a wedding. Will I wear a satin or silk dress with all frills and things, just like a princess?" she had asked, and Susan had replied, "My darling you can wear whatever you like as long as it's in a pastel colour. Absolutely no purples or magentas though, young lady. Your grandma can help you choose, okay?"

Rose and Abby had chosen a beautiful apricot coloured short sleeved, full waisted, below the knee, dress, simple but perfect for the occasion. Abby had loved it and couldn't wait to be a bridesmaid.

Tom was as nonchalant as ever about the whole wedding, but Rose had made up for his lack of enthusiasm by being thrilled to see her dear friend finally settle down with such a lovely man as Ian Green. She just knew that he would make Susan very happy.

At 3:00 pm, Rose left Tom and Abby watching the women's singles final at Wimbledon together on the TV. They were under strict instructions to be at The Little Inn for 4:30 pm. The wedding was scheduled to start at 5:00 pm.

She drove around to Susan's condo in her old Volvo. It was a beautiful day; the sky was an azure blue, and the temperature wasn't too hot. It was just a perfect day for a wedding.

When Rose knocked on Susan's door, she was greeted by her friend wrapped in a big white fluffy bath towel.

"Come in, Rose, I've just been soaking in the hot- tub. Are you ready for a glass of wine?"

Rose laughed, "Oh Susan, you and your hot-tub. Yes, I'd love a glass of wine."

Fluffy, Susan's cat, had sidled up to Rose and had entwined herself between her legs making it impossible for Rose to walk.

"Hey there, Fluffy, you want some attention, do you?" Rose said and lifted the furry feline up and cuddled her gently.

"Are you sure Olive is alright with looking after Fluffy while you're gone? We don't mind having her. Abby would absolutely love to have a cat to play with."

"Well, Olive was quite insistent, but I'll leave your telephone number with her in case Fluffy becomes too much of a burden."

Olive was Ian's aged mother who, up until a year ago, had run an egg farm single handedly until Susan had moved in and helped her. She now lived at Harbour Hill retirement home and absolutely loved her new home. Olive was 96 years old and still as independent and feisty as she had been twenty years ago.

"So, dear friend, you said you wanted to talk to me about something? Fire away before we go upstairs to get you ready for your big day."

Susan looked uncomfortable; she had had time to think about Ian's idea of moving and although she loved her condo a new place together did make sense, she would still have her hot tub and Fluffy, but if moving to Goderich made Ian happy, then that's what they would do. She started to tell Rose about the potential move, and she could see by Rose's face that she too had mixed feelings.

"Susan, I'll miss not having you around the corner in the village, but I do really see Ian's point of view and it will be super exciting house hunting. I'm assuming that you haven't started looking yet. It may take some time, but I'm excited for you both. Don't dwell on it too much though and certainly don't let it affect your honeymoon. Just think, by tomorrow you'll be in romantic Paris, the city of love. Put all your cares behind you and swallow up the Parisian air. Okay, enough talk, now it's time to go upstairs and prepare you for your big day. Let's do it and forget about your moving, tomorrow's another day, you can think about it then."

The two friends went upstairs together. Rose, although she had visited Susan dozens of times before, had never actually been upstairs. They entered Susans bedroom and the first thing that struck Rose was the giant king-sized bed. It was a spacious room, very modern with beige carpet everywhere even in the bathroom. The room was sparsely furnished with just the giant bed and two side tables plus a table holding a metal sculpture. A white cotton spread covered the bed and white blinds graced the windows. It all looked like something out of a magazine, 'Homes and Gardens', maybe.

Rose thought about her and Tom's bedroom which she loved but was totally the opposite to Susans pristine room. In their bedroom the walls were painted a soft yellow, and pictures of the family were hung all over the walls. Their bed was covered in a colourful batik cloth with scatter cushions and Bens's dog bed sat at the foot of their bed looking a bit worse for wear these days. On their bedside tables were mounds of books and on Roses side there were more books stacked on the floor, but Rose loved their bedroom and looked forward every night to cozying up in bed with one of her books and of course, with Tom.

The small table by the bedroom door was home to a metal sculpture. Rose looked at it and was trying to work out what it was when Susan laughed out loud. "You're admiring my sculpture I see. It's meant to be two lovers entwined as one. I love it. It was a present to me from Henri." Deep sadness misted over Susan's eyes as she remembered her fiancé, Henri le Bruin, her dashing French officer from Quebec who had been shot fatally all those years ago.

How many years ago was that? Susan thought, "it had to be at least 10 years.

Rose's eyes landed on the cream silk, off the shoulder wedding dress hanging from the wardrobe door. It was exquisitely sewed with little seed pearls inlaid in lace. The cream silk would complement Susan's auburn hair and her lightly freckled skin. She will look divine, Rose thought.

"How are you going to wear your hair? Up or down?"

"I thought about wearing it up in a chignon, but you know something, Rose, Ian loves my hair just loose. I've got a white lace mantilla which I bought in Rome and used whenever we went into a church. I thought that I might wear that, I'll see what it looks like when I'm in my dress."

Susan had whipped off her towel wrapping and was putting on some cream lace underwear when they both heard a dull thud coming from the hallway, followed by a couple of creeks on the stairs.

Susan put her finger to her mouth and indicated to Rose to creep into the wardrobe, while she herself ran to her bedside table, opened the drawer, and pulled out a small silver pistol. She looked out of her bedroom window. There was a grey Kia car that looked remarkably like Jane Smith's. Susan ran to the adjoining bathroom. It was a 'Jack and Jill' affair with access to both the guest room and the master suite. Because of the carpeted flooring, Susan was able to move silently into the guest room where she crouched behind the bedroom door. The squeak of the landing flooring indicated that the predator was about to enter her bedroom. Susan prayed that Rose would remain hidden in the wardrobe, she knew that once her bedroom had been checked out the intruder would surely move to the guest room. She held her gun out ready to shoot. The door to the guest room moved silently open, a man totally dressed in black and wearing a black Balaclava, entered. Susan jumped forward and yelled out, "Hands up or I'll shoot."

The man holding a small submachine gun turned and was about to let blast when there was a cry like a wild banshee as Rose rushed into the room holding the metal sculpture above her head and brought it heavily down upon the head of the masked man. He collapsed at once and as Susan stood over him holding her small gun, Rose whipped off his balaclava to reveal his identity. He was a good-looking man with a very square jawline. Both Susan and Rose had seen the artist's impression of Eli Klassen but had never met the man in person.

They had caught the man who had murdered Susan's niece.

"Susan, do you have any zip-ties? We'll need to secure this man before he comes to." Rose asked nervously as Eli started to moan and regain consciousness.

"Better yet I've got these handcuffs." Susan marched back to her bedroom and over to her bedside table, opened the drawer, and pulled out a pair of black painted handcuffs with little satin ribbons tied to the cuffs, she ran back to Eli and clamped his wrists together with the handcuffs. They wouldn't hold him for long as they were purely for recreational use, but hopefully long enough. It surely wouldn't take DCI Whitaker more than fifteen minutes to get to her place from Clinton, although, glancing at her watch, Susan realized that Jeff would probably not be in Clinton, but at his home in London.

Having made the phone call to Jeff, Rose looked at Susan still standing with just her cream lace underwear on and nothing else. She had to laugh, on this day of all days, they had caught themselves a killer and with this in mind Rose said, "Come on, dear friend, get yourself dressed, we've got a wedding to go to."

The two of them went back to the bedroom and Rose lifted the beautiful dress off the hanger.

Susan had walked over to the window and was peering out. The grey Kia car was still parked in front of her house.

"Rose, I think we have more company."

Just as Susan said that a squeak could be heard out on the landing. This time there was no time to prepare. Susan picked up her gun, and Rose grabbed the metal sculpture. Both women hid behind the bedroom door.

Slowly the door started to move open to reveal Jane Smith standing in the opening, a small pistol in her hand. She had obviously not yet gone into the guest bedroom and therefore had not discovered the unconscious handcuffed body of Eli, her brother.

Susan stepped out and pointed her gun directly at Jane's back.

'Don't move or I'll shoot."

Jane turned her head and was greeted with the sight of Susan scantily clad in just her lacey underwear, and Rose, wearing a beautiful peach coloured sheaf dress and holding over her head a large metal sculpture.

"Lower your gun now." Susan shouted.

Jane lowered her gun and Susan rushed forward and took it from her.

"Now, go and sit on the bed, and don't try anything silly"

Susan turned to Rose and said, "Rose, downstairs in the kitchen you'll find a roll of duct tape, I think it's on top of the microwave. Can you fetch it for me. We need to tie Jane up while we wait for the police."

Rose went downstairs to find the tape leaving Susan alone with Jane.

"Right, before I tape up your mouth, I'd like you to tell me why you killed my niece, Mary?"

Jane looked defiant, and then softened up, "Firstly, I want to know what you've done to Eli, my brother?"

"Oh, he's tied up in the guest room. He's not going anywhere. The police are on their way. But answer me this, were you responsible for my niece's murder?"

Jane thought before she answered.

"It was Eli's idea to kill her. You see she walked in on me packing the mink pelts with drugs."

"Hold on, back up a minute", Susan said, "What do you mean by mink pelts and drugs? This is news to me."

"Oh, I see that you're not quite in the loop then. Well, it doesn't matter, I'm sure you'll find out soon."

"Tell me now or I'll shoot you in your leg and believe me, I mean it." Susan snarled, she'd had enough of Jane Smith and now she was angry. It was her wedding day, for God's sake.

"Alright, don't get snarly, I'll tell you."

Rose entered the room holding a roll of duct tape in her hand. "I'll go and tape up Eli's wrists and feet and tape up his mouth" she said aware that Susan was breathing hard and looked quite scary. "I'll be back in a minute, okay?"

"Right, tell me about the drugs and why you killed Mary."

Jane fidgeted with her hands and kicked her feet, but Susan held her gun firmly at her. Finally, Jane settled and began to relay the story of setting up the mink farm and using it as a vehicle to traffic drugs.

"You see, when Eli came back from South Africa it was clear that his energies had to be channelled somewhere as he was so restless. The Wiebe brother's farm seemed the perfect location and both brothers were quite malleable.

Also, having worked at the Varna mink farm all those years ago, I had a working knowledge of the business. The drug side of it came naturally from our sister, Lydia. She had a ready list of willing suppliers, mostly from B.C.

Mary knew nothing about our operation and had only met Eli socially once before when he visited me unexpectedly, and Mary was having tea with me at the time. Funnily enough Mary couldn't remember Eli even though she grew up with him as a neighbour all those years ago on Bronsen Line. He had gone out to South Africa about the same time as Samuel and she had eloped and then she had not seen him since.

At first when she found me in my garage packing up the mink pelts, she was excited. You see, both of us had worked at the Varna mink farm many years ago and she thought that I was just selling the pelts. I wasn't sure if she had even seen the packages of drugs, she never mentioned them but, when I told Eli what had happened, he said that she could spoil the whole business, and that she had to go. I never realized that he meant 'go' as in being killed. My brother has always had a sadistic streak in him. That's why he became a mercenary, but I swear that I never asked him to kill Mary."

"And what about the note I received from the Book of Exodus, was that you or Eli?"

"It was Eli's idea, you see he'd become quite religious while living in South Africa. Anyway, we both were angry when we heard that our niece, Isabelle had died horribly in that awful Venezuelan prison. The 'eye for an eye', commandment seemed apt to us, you lose a niece just as we have lost our Isabelle."

"Was the murder at the golf course planned too or did Eli take it upon himself to kill Mary then?"

Jane went quiet, but then answered Susan with a low voice, almost a mumble.

"Eli knew that we were going to play golf that morning because I had told him so, but as to the logistics, I never knew that he was going to do it then. I was as shocked as everyone. It was horrible and I'll never forgive Eli for doing that right in front of me."

Susan could hear police sirens getting closer. Rose had returned with the duct tape and Eli was beginning to groan next door in the guest room. Susan looked at her watch. They had just ten minutes before they were due at The Little Inn. Quickly securing Jane's wrists and ankles, the final flourish was a large strip of duct tape over her mouth, she said to Rose,

"Help me with my dress Rose and then we must go. I cannot be late for my wedding."

Rose glanced at her watch. They had only a short time to get ready, but it was, after all, quite fashionable to be a little late for one's own wedding.

"Isn't it an offence to leave the scene of a crime?" she tentatively said.

"Well, I certainly am not going to miss my wedding. Listen, the police are very close, they'll be here any minute now and hopefully we'll be able to explain what went on. Actually, Rose, could you speak to DCI Whittaker for me while I get dressed. "

Rose nodded and tapped in Jeffs cell number. She watched as Susan slid the beautiful dress over her head and stood back to admire herself in the mirror. Rose mouthed the word, "Amazing', just as Jeff answered his phone. Rose could tell that he was on his motor bike and using his earpiece from the background noise. She had to shout so that he could hear her.

"Oh, thank God you answered," Rose said, "Look, Jeff, it's Susan's wedding day and we must leave immediately, or she'll be late. We can hear sirens in the distance, but we're afraid that they won't be here in time because we seriously do have to leave the house now. You can find us at the Little Inn, and we will be available to answer all your questions if you let us attend the service first."

DCI Whittaker smiled to himself. Rose Blair certainly sounded desperate and well she should as it was her friend's wedding day. He answered quickly.

"Calm down, Rose. I understand your predicament and yes, of course you must leave now for Susan's wedding. I gather from your first call that both Eli and Jane Klassen have been securely tied up and that they both tried to attack Susan? Am I correct?"

"Yes, on both counts, although attack is putting it mildly. They were out to kill Susan, and I would have been co-lateral damage too. Now, we must go. Sorry about this, but we have at least caught your killers for you."

"Yes, that you have. Go off with you and enjoy the special day, oh, and thank you to both of you."

Rose ended the call and stood back to look at her friend who was just brushing her hair.

"Come on, MS Parker, it's time for your big day. By the way, you look gorgeous."

"Okay, I'm ready. Now let's go, Ian will be getting nervous if I'm much later."

They both got into Rose's old car and drove off, not quite as fast as if they were in Susan's Porsche, but still faster than Rose usually drove.

Just as Rose and Susan were leaving Harbour Court, two police cars screeched around the corner, sirens blaring and blue lights flashing. Rose kept on driving and headed for Main Street and the Little Inn. Nothing was going to stop them now, her friend would make her wedding and she herself, would be united with Tom and Abby.

Life was sweet and there was nothing better than a wedding to count your blessings. Rose knew just how blessed she was to have such a wonderful husband like Tom, and an adorable grand daughter, Abby, and, of course, blessed to have survived the attack on Susan and herself.

It was a sobering thought had things turned out differently, but she wasn't going to give reign to those thoughts right now. Today was a time for love and union, for trust and loyalty and that right now was all Rose wished for her friend and, indeed, for all couples old or young.

They arrived at the Little Inn and Susan walked confidently into the main restaurant area which had been set up for the wedding. Ian turned around just as she entered the room, and his face lit up like a beacon. Rose could see the look of love written all over his face and she just knew that everything was going to be alright.

www.ingramcontent.com/pod-product-compliance
Lightning Source LLC
Chambersburg PA
CBHW070343260626
47160CB00003B/1124